"I Never Had Any Intention Of Bullying You, Miss Sullivan."

Tori tried not to watch the soft curve of his lips as he spoke to her, but he was so close she had little choice. She remembered how she'd once fantasized about kissing those lips. Of course, that was before he turned on her and threw her out of his company onto her rear end. The surge of anger doused the old memories as her gaze met his.

"What then?" she asked, her voice laced with sarcasm. "Were you going to take your friend's suggestion and seduce me? Certainly you're so masterful in the bedroom that one good romp would change my mind, right?"

Wade moved a fraction of an inch closer to her. For a moment, Tori tensed, thinking he might be leaning in to kiss her. She wanted him to, and she didn't. She pressed a gentle hand to his chest. She could feel his heart racing just as quickly as her own. He was not immune to his own game.

They were both playing with fire.

Dear Reader,

I'm so excited to share this book with you. *Undeniable Demands* kicks off my very first series—Secrets of Eden. When I first started writing for Harlequin Desire, I immersed myself in the world of wealthy, powerful alpha males. My first two heroes had family money to help them start their business empires, so this time I wanted to write some self-made heroes. I wanted a group of men who had defied the odds, overcome tragedy and made themselves into the sexy alpha heroes that Desire readers know and love.

But everyone has some baggage from their past, and the heroes of Secrets of Eden are no exception. The foster brothers share a dark secret that threatens not only their family and their livelihood but their chance to find love. At the same time, their secret is what brings Wade and Victoria together. And boy, do the sparks fly! The spunky environmental architect isn't about to make anything easy for Wade, and it was fun to write about their tempestuous relationship.

I can't wait for you to fall in love with the whole Eden family, as I have. If you enjoy Wade and Tori's story, tell me by visiting my website at www.andrealaurence.com, like my fan page on Facebook or follow me on Twitter. I love to hear from my readers!

Enjoy!

Andrea

ANDREA LAURENCE

UNDENIABLE DEMANDS

HARLEQUIN®

entertain, enrich, inspire™

Recycling programs
for this product may
not exist in your area.

ISBN-13: 978-0-373-73220-3

UNDENIABLE DEMANDS

Copyright © 2013 by Andrea Laurence

This edition published by arrangement with Harlequin Books S.A.

For questions and comments about the quality of this book please contact us
at CustomerService@Harlequin.com.

® and TM are trademarks of Harlequin Enterprises Limited or its corporate
affiliates. Trademarks indicated with ® are registered in the United States Patent
and Trademark Office, the Canadian Trade Marks Office and in other countries.

www.Harlequin.com

Printed in U.S.A.

Books by Andrea Laurence

Harlequin Desire

What Lies Beneath #2152
More Than He Expected #2172
*Undeniable Demands #2207

*Secrets of Eden

Other titles by this author available in ebook format.

ANDREA LAURENCE

has been a lover of reading and writing stories since she learned her ABCs. She always dreamed of seeing her work in print and is thrilled to finally be able to share her books with the world. A dedicated West Coast girl transplanted to the Deep South, she's working on her own "happily ever after" with her boyfriend and their collection of animals that shed like nobody's business. You can contact Andrea at her website, www.andrealaurence.com.

To Vicki Lewis Thompson, Rhonda Nelson
and Kira Sinclair

You're the best plotting partners a girl could have.
You helped me take the smallest kernel of an idea
and develop it into a great multibook series.
I look forward to many more years of creativity,
laughter and good food with my ladies.

One

Wade hated the snow. Always had. You'd think a man born and raised in New England would feel differently or leave, but he'd done neither. Every November when the first few flakes started falling, a part of his soul would shrivel up until spring. That was why he'd booked himself a trip to Jamaica for the week before Christmas. He'd planned to return to the Edens', as always, for the holiday, but the frantic call he'd received from his foster sister, Julianne, had changed everything.

He had been loath to tell his assistant to cancel the trip, but perhaps if all went well, he could use the reservation after Christmas. He could ring in the New Year on a beach, drinking something frothy, with thoughts of his troubles buried deep.

Interesting choice of words.

The BMW SUV wound its way down the two-lane

road that led to the Garden of Eden Christmas Tree Farm. Wade preferred to drive his roadster, but rural Connecticut in winter was just not the place for it, so he'd left it in Manhattan. The SUV had snow tires, chains in the back and enough clearance not to scrape on chunks of ice in poorly cleared areas.

Spying the large red apple-shaped sign that marked the entrance to his foster parents' Christmas tree farm, Wade breathed a sigh of relief. He hadn't realized until that moment that he'd been holding his breath. Even under the less-than-ideal circumstances, returning home always made him feel better.

The farm was the only home he'd ever really had. None of the other foster homes had felt like one. He had no warm memories of living with his great-aunt before that, nor of his early years with his mother. But the Garden of Eden was just that: paradise. Especially for an abandoned young boy who could just as easily have become a career criminal as a millionaire in real estate.

The Edens changed everything. For him and every other child who had come to live there. He owed that couple his life. They were his parents, without question. Wade didn't know who his father was and had only seen his mother once since she dropped him at her aunt's doorstep as a toddler. When he thought of home and family, he thought of the farm and the family the Edens had pulled together.

They were able to have only one child of their own, their daughter, Julianne. For a time it seemed that their dreams of a house bustling with children who would help on the farm and one day take over the family business had been dashed. But then they decided to renovate an old barn into a bunkhouse perfect for rowdy boys and started taking in foster children.

Wade had been the first. Julianne had been in pig-tails when he arrived, dragging her favorite doll behind her. Wade had been in his share of foster homes, and this time just felt different. He was not a burden. Not a way to get a check from the state. He was their son.

Which is why he wished he was visiting them for another reason. In his own mind, disappointing his parents would be the greatest sin he could commit. Even worse than the one he'd committed fifteen years ago that got him into this mess.

Wade turned the SUV into the driveway, then by-passed the parking lot and took the small road behind their large Federal-style house to where the family kept their cars. It was nearing the middle of the afternoon on a Friday, but even so, there were at least ten customer cars in the lot. It was December 21—only a few days until Christmas. His mother, Molly, would be in the gift shop, pushing sugar cookies, cider and hot choco-late on folks while they waited for Ken or one of the employees to haul and bag their new tree.

Wade felt the sudden, familiar urge to start trimming trees and hauling them out to people's cars. He'd done it for all of his teenage years and every Christmas break from Yale. It came naturally to want to jump back into the work. But first things first. He had to take care of the business that had brought him here instead of the warm beaches of Jamaica.

Julianne's call had been unexpected. None of the kids were very good about calling or visiting their par-ents or each other like they should. They were all busy, all successful, the way the Edens had wanted them to be. But their success also made it easy to forget to make time for the important people in their lives.

When Julianne had shown up at the farm for Thanksgiving with little warning, she'd been in for quite the surprise. Their father, Ken, was recovering from a heart attack. They hadn't called any of the kids because they didn't want them worrying about it or the crippling hospital bills.

Wade, Heath, Xander, Brody—any of the boys could've written a check and taken care of their problems, but Ken and Molly insisted they had it under control. Unfortunately, their solution was to sell a few plots of land they couldn't use for growing trees. They couldn't understand why the kids were so upset. And of course, the kids couldn't tell their parents the truth. That secret needed to remain buried in the past. And Wade was here to make sure it stayed that way.

If he was lucky, he could take one of the four-wheelers out to the property, buy the land back from the new owner and return before Molly could start wondering what he was up to. He wouldn't keep the purchase a secret from his parents, but he'd certainly rather they not fret over the whole situation until it was done.

Wade found the house empty, as expected. He left a note on the worn kitchen table, slipped into his heavy coat and boots and went out to grab one of the four-wheelers. He could've driven his SUV, but he didn't want to pull up in an expensive car and start waving money around at people.

Heath and Brody had both made visits to the farm since Julianne broke the news. Digging up as much information as they could, they found out that the person who had bought the smallest parcel of land was already living out there in some kind of camper. That sounded positive to him. They might need the money more than the land. But if they thought some rich guy was bullying them to sell it, they'd clamp down. Or jack up the price.

Wade took the four-wheeler down the well-worn path that went through the center of the farm. After selling eighty-five acres, the Edens still had two hundred acres left. Almost all of it was populated with balsam and Fraser fir trees. The northeastern portion of the property was sloped and rocky. They'd never had much success planting trees out there, so he'd understood why Ken had opted to sell it. He just wished his father hadn't.

By the time he rounded a corner on the trail and neared the border of the Edens' property, it was a little after two-thirty. The sky was clear and blue and the sun's rays pounded down on the snow, making it nearly blinding despite his sunglasses. He slowed and pulled out the new surveyor's map Brody had downloaded. The eighty-five acres that his parents had sold were split into two large tracts and one small one. Comparing the map to the GPS location on his phone, he could tell that just over the rise was the smallest, a ten-acre residential property. He was fairly certain this was the one he was after.

Wade refolded the map and looked around for any familiar landmarks. He'd deliberately chosen a spot he would remember. There had been a crooked maple tree and a rock that looked like a giant turtle. He scanned the landscape, but it appeared to him as though all the trees were crooked, and all the rocks were buried under a foot of snow. It was impossible to know for sure if this chunk of the property was the right one.

Damn. He'd thought for certain that he would know the spot when he saw it. That night fifteen years ago remained etched in his memory no matter how hard he tried to forget it. It was one of those moments that changes your whole life. Where you make a decision, right or wrong, and have to live with it forever.

Still, Wade was certain this was the right area. He didn't remember traveling far enough to reach the other plots. He'd been in too big a hurry to roam around the property all night trying to find the perfect spot. He eyed another maple tree, this one more crooked than the others. That had to be the one. He'd just have to buy the land back and hope that once spring came around, he would find the turtle rock at its base and know he'd bought the right plot.

Surging forward through the snow, he continued up to the rise and then started descending into the clearing toward what looked like some sort of shimmering silver mirage.

He pulled closer and realized it was the midafternoon sun reflecting off the superbly polished aluminum siding of an old Airstream trailer. You could have got a suntan from the rays coming off that thing. Parked beside it was an old Ford pickup truck with dually tires to haul the twenty-foot monster of a camper.

Wade stopped and killed the engine on the four-wheeler. There was no sign of life from inside the camper yet. Brody had searched online for the property sale records and found the new owner was V. A. Sullivan. Cornwall was a fairly small town, and he didn't remember any Sullivans when he went to school, so they must be new to the area. That was just as well. He didn't need to deal with anyone who remembered his troublesome days before the Edens and might give him grief.

His boots crunched through the snow until he reached the rounded doorway. It had a small window in it that he watched for movement when he knocked. Nothing. No sound of people inside, either.

Just great. He'd come all the way out here for nothing.

Wade was about to turn and head back home when he heard the telltale click of a shotgun safety. His head spun to the left, following the sound, and he found himself in the sights. The woman was standing about twenty feet away, bundled just as heavily as he was in a winter coat with a knit cap and sunglasses hiding most of her features. Long strands of fiery red hair peeked out from her hat and blew in the chilly wind. The distinctive color immediately caught his eye. He'd known a woman with hair that color a long time ago. It had been beautiful, like liquid flames. Appropriate, since he was playing with fire now.

On reflex, his hands went up. Getting shot by some overprotective, rural militia type was not on his agenda for the day. "Hey, there," he called out, trying to sound as friendly and nonthreatening as he could.

The woman hesitated, and then the shotgun dropped slightly. "Can I help you?"

"Are you Mrs. Sullivan?" Hopefully Mr. Sullivan wasn't out in the woods with a shotgun of his own.

"*Miss* Sullivan," she corrected. "What's it to you?"

A single female. Even better. Wade had a certain charm about him that served him well with the fairer sex. He smiled widely. "My name is Wade Mitchell. I wanted to talk to you about possibly—"

"Arrogant, pigheaded real-estate developer Wade Mitchell?" The woman took a few steps forward.

Wade frowned. She didn't seem to care for him at all. He wished to God the woman wasn't so bundled up so he could see who she was. Maybe then he could figure out why the mention of his name seemed to agitate her. Of course, he was wearing just as much winter gear as she was. "Yes, ma'am, although I wouldn't go so far as to use those adjectives. I wanted to see if you would be interested in..."

His words dropped off as the shotgun rose again. "Aw, hell," she lamented. "I thought it looked kinda like you under all those layers, but I thought, why would Wade Mitchell be in Cornwall making my life hell again after all this time?"

Wade's eyes widened behind his dark sunglasses. "I have no intention of making your life hell, Miss Sullivan."

"Get off my land."

"I'm sorry, have I done something to you?" He scanned his brain. Had he dated a Sullivan? Beaten up her brother? He had no memory of what he could've done to piss this woman off so badly.

The woman stomped across the snow, closing the gap between them with the gun still pointed directly at him. She pulled off her sunglasses to study him more closely, revealing a lovely heart-shaped face and pale eyes. Her skin was creamy, the perfect backdrop to the fiery strands of hair framing her face. When her blue eyes met his, he noticed a challenge there, as though she was daring him not to remember her.

Fortunately, Wade had an excellent memory. One good enough to know that he was in trouble. The fiery redhead glaring at him was a hard woman to forget. He'd certainly tried over the years, but from time to time, she'd slipped into his subconscious and haunted his dreams with her piercing, ice-blue gaze. A gaze that reflected the hurt of betrayal that he couldn't understand.

Property owner V. A. Sullivan was none other than Victoria Sullivan: green architect, eco-warrior and the employee he'd fired from his company seven years ago.

His stomach instantly sank. Of all the people who could've bought this property, it had to be her. Victoria Sullivan. The first person he'd ever fired from his company. It had pained him at the time, but he'd really had no choice. He had a strict policy on ethics violations. She hadn't taken the news well. And judging by her stiff posture and tightly gripped firearm, she was still upset about it.

"Victoria!" he said with a wide smile, trying to sound pleasantly surprised to see her after all this time. "I had no idea you were living out here now."

"Miss Sullivan," she corrected.

Wade nodded. "Of course. Could you please drop the gun? I'm unarmed."

"You won't be when the cops come." Her words were as icy cold as the snow, but eventually the gun disengaged and dropped to her side.

She pushed past him to the front door of the Airstream, pulling it open and climbing the stairs. "What do you want, Mr. Mitchell?"

As she hung at the top of the steps, looking back at him, Wade realized he needed to change his tactic, and fast. His original plan had been to tell the owner that he wanted the property for one of his development projects. If he told her that, she'd refuse him just to ruin his plans.

He'd have to appeal to a different side of her. That is, if he could explain himself before she started shooting.

"Miss Sullivan, I'd like to buy back this property from you."

* * *

Tori hung on the steps, the rage slowly uncoiling in her belly. This man was determined to ruin everything she held dear. He had taken away her reputation and very nearly her career. His turning on her suddenly had also damaged her ability to trust men. Out of the blue, he'd accused her of terrible things and tossed her out. She'd lost her first real apartment after he fired her.

And now that she was trying to settle down and establish herself again, he wanted to destroy her plans for her dream home. She just knew it. Her jaw set firmly, she made her decision before he even asked the question. If he were on fire, she wouldn't bother to spit on him.

"It's not for sale." She slipped inside and let the door slam behind her.

She was pulling off her coat, about to toss it onto the foldout bed, when she heard the door of the trailer open behind her. Tori spun on her heel and found the bastard standing in her tiny kitchen. He'd slipped out of his winter coat and tugged off his hat as he entered. He stood there now in a pair of dress pants and a plaid button-down shirt. The hunter-green of the top made his own green eyes seem even darker and more intriguing than she remembered. Because of the stocking cap he'd worn, his short, dark brown hair was messier than she'd ever seen it.

Without his slick suits and perfect hair, he looked nothing like the real-estate giant who had ruled over his company from the top floor. But he still had a commanding presence. She'd forgotten how tall he was: at least six foot two, with a powerful build. The large man seemed to take up all the space in her trailer, which had always had the perfect amount of room for her. It was as though he'd sucked up all the air, making her oddly warm and her camper uncomfortably small.

And she hated that about him.

Without hesitating, she picked up her shotgun again. Truthfully, it was loaded with shells full of recycled rubber pellets. She carried it with her to the compost bin in case she needed to scare off any foraging critters. She'd caught a black bear in the bin last week. The rubber pellets would send animals scurrying without seriously hurting them. Hopefully it would do the same with Wade Mitchell.

"Do you mind stepping back outside? I spent a lot of money to renovate this trailer and I'm not going to ruin it by shooting you in here."

Wade had only a momentary flash of alarm in his eyes before he smiled at her in a way that made her cheeks flush and her knees weaken. She remembered feeling that way whenever he would walk down the hallway past her cubicle and greet her with "good morning." She'd been fresh out of college and in awe of the two young mavericks with their up-and-coming real-estate development company. Alex Stanton was the golden playboy, but she was instantly drawn to the darker, more serious Wade. Then and now, his wide grin and strong, aristocratic features usually got him his way.

If she wasn't careful, she might fall prey to them again. She knew better than to trust a guy like him.

"Miss Sullivan, can we please talk about this without you constantly threatening to shoot me?"

"There's nothing to talk about." Tori kept the gun in one hand while she pulled off her hat and scarf with the other. She was burning up, and it had nothing to do with her new propane heating system. It was Wade and her overheated and long-ignored libido. She hated that the man who'd betrayed and fired her could still send her pulse racing after all this time. "And it's rude to come inside uninvited, so you deserve to be shot."

"I apologize," he said, laying his coat across the bench seat of her dining table. "But it is imperative that I discuss this with you today."

Oh, she was sure it was. No doubt he had bought the forty-acre property beside her and wanted her additional ten to add to whatever ridiculous project he was developing out here. There might be an army of backhoes and land movers over the horizon just waiting for her to sign off so they could start their work. But she wasn't giving up this land. This purchase had been years in the making. Her genealogy research had been what lured her up here, but from the first time she'd set foot in the area, she knew this was where she wanted to build her home.

Finding out the Edens were selling some property had been the chance of a lifetime. The lot was perfect. It sloped down, slightly, but would allow her to design a stilted, multistory home that had a living room with a wide vista of windows overlooking the valley below. Being surrounded by two hundred acres of tree farm on two sides guaranteed she wouldn't have a strip mall out her back door anytime soon.

She had a couple months in between projects to start designing and building her house. It was the perfect opportunity just when she had the time and money to jump on it. And he couldn't have it.

"I know that you're used to getting your way, Mr. Mitchell, but I'm afraid it isn't going to happen this time."

On cue, her electric teapot began to chirp on the

counter and spit out steam. She'd turned it on before she'd stepped out to put some trash in her compost bin, and now it was ready for her to extend some unintended hospitality. When she turned to look at Wade again, he had seated himself at her dining-table booth, a look of smug expectation in his eyes.

With a sigh, she set down the shotgun. It was hard to make tea when you were holding a heavy, loaded firearm.

"May I ask how much you paid for the land?"

"You may not, although I'm sure it's public record somewhere if you take the time to have one of the corporate minions you haven't fired look for it." She pulled out two teacups from her bamboo plywood cabinet above the sink. She shook her loose leaf tea into two infusers, put them in the cups and poured the hot water over them.

"My guess would be about a hundred and twenty-five thousand. There're no utilities run out here yet."

Tori refused to look at him. Of course the real estate guy could nail the price within a few thousand dollars. "What's your point?"

"My point is that I'll offer you double what you paid for it."

At that, Tori fumbled the jar of organic honey and sent it crashing to the Marmoleum floor. Fortunately, it didn't shatter. She quickly crouched down to grab it, but he had reached out for it as well and beat her to it. He held out the jar to her. Tori looked down at him, only inches away, and felt a familiar and unwelcome tingle deep in her belly. When she took the jar from his hand, her fingers brushed his and the tingle turned into a surge right to her core.

Jerking upright as though she'd been burned by his

touch, she quickly recovered and removed the infusers, then added a dollop of the honey to each cup. She plunked his tea down in front of him and took a seat on the opposite side of the table.

"That's ridiculous." She said the words knowing she meant both her reaction to him and his offer for her land. Tori knew better than to let herself fall for Wade's good looks or his seemingly good offer.

"Maybe. But that's what I'm offering."

"You're hiding something," she accused. "You're the guy who built your business buying cheap buildings and flipping them for a fortune. No way you'd pay one penny more than is necessary to turn a profit on whatever project you're wanting to build out here."

Wade turned to look her in the eye. A lock of brown hair had fallen into his face, giving him a boyish charm she had to steel her resolve against. "I'm not building anything out here. This isn't about money."

Tori scoffed. "You don't get to be a millionaire before you're thirty unless you're born into money or driven by it. Either way, everything is about money."

Wade watched her. He took a sip of his tea before he answered. "This is about family. That's more important to me than even money. This property belonged to my parents. They sold it without telling me or my other siblings. We never would've let them do that if we'd known. They worked too hard their whole lives for this land. We grew up here. Our childhood was here. If we'd known they were having financial problems, I would've taken care of things before they resorted to this."

Tori felt herself being sucked in by his story. The expression on his handsome face was one of sincere concern. The words sounded so convincing. But this was the same man who had praised her potential and work ethic, then fired her the next day. Ryan had also seemed sincere, and nearly every word out of his mouth over the past two years had been a lie.

She had been raised with a naive spirit by hippies who wanted only to experience life and culture. They didn't have a malicious bone in their bodies and never thought other people did, either.

Life had taught Tori differently. Wade had taught her differently. He had heard her pleas of innocence and turned his back on them. He hadn't believed her. So why should she believe him now?

The people who had sold her this land—Molly and Ken Eden—were a very sweet older couple. No way they'd spawned a son like Mitchell. They didn't even have the same last name. It wasn't even a well-planned lie. She wanted to be insulted by his lack of faith in her ability to see through his crap. Did he think she would just melt into a puddle at his feet the minute he knocked on the door and flashed those deep green eyes at her? Or started waving cash?

She didn't need Wade's money. She'd paid cash for this property. She was one of the most highly sought after green architects in America. She'd traveled thousands of miles in this Airstream to build environmentally friendly buildings, homes and businesses. Tori had several large and successful projects in Seattle, Santa Fe and San Francisco. She was wrapping up one in Philadelphia just after the first of the year. She did well enough that she could laugh at his offer. But it couldn't hurt to push him and see how far he was willing to take this.

"What if I said I would sell it back to you for half a million?" There was no way the land was worth that much unless there was oil, gold or diamonds hidden beneath her feet. She doubted it, though. She'd never heard of Wade Mitchell being interested in any of those things. The only thing about land he cared for was what he could build on top of it.

Wade didn't even flinch. "I would get out my checkbook and sign on the dotted line so you could find an even better piece of land and everyone would be happy. Let me assure you that nothing is more important than preserving my family and my history."

Wow. He was certainly desperate for this land. She almost felt bad for him. Any other person might have immediately given in and made his day. Four times the value was a great offer. A crazy offer. One that she was probably crazy to turn down. Even with her success, half a million was quite a lump of cash. Tori could certainly do a lot with it: buy new land, build her dream house without a mortgage attached to it, get a new hybrid pickup truck. She had to admit, if it were any other person sitting across the table from her, she'd probably take the money and tow her trailer off into the sunset.

But it wasn't any other person. It was Wade Mitchell. And she wasn't about to sell him this land. Not for any price. Just because it was worth it to watch him squirm. This would be as close to payback as she would ever get. It was his bad luck that he wanted *her* land.

"You're really quite good," she said, nodding and watching her tea instead of his handsome face. She wouldn't let herself get pulled in and swayed by his mesmerizing eyes and fabricated sob story. She'd already caught herself being a sucker once this year, and that was enough. Maybe if he came around in a few weeks, she'd let him be her dumb mistake of the New

Year. "Did you practice that speech long or was that off the cuff?"

Wade stiffened, pushing the half-empty cup of tea aside and shelving the charm. "Is all this animosity over your termination years ago?"

Now it was Tori's turn to stiffen in her chair. He made her seem petty for holding that over him all these years later. "Absolutely. I don't take affronts to my reputation lightly."

"You weren't worried about your reputation when you slept with one of our suppliers and put my company in jeopardy."

"I didn't sleep with anybody. I told you then that I didn't do any of the things you accused me of. Nothing has changed. Just because you didn't believe me doesn't mean I wasn't telling the truth."

"They were serious charges, and I needed to deal with them as such. I did what I had to do."

"And I'm doing what I have to do. I'm keeping this land. It's mine. Whether or not I like you or resent what you did is irrelevant."

"This isn't about me or you and your damaged pride. This is about Ken and Molly Eden and everything they worked for. I want to give them back what's rightfully theirs."

Tori straightened and shot him as lethal a gaze as she could manage. "You mean, *mine*. I signed those papers at the lawyer's office two months ago. I didn't hold a gun to their heads and make them sell me this land."

"Wouldn't have surprised me if you did," he said bitterly, glancing over at the shotgun sitting on the counter.

"They sold it all on their own. I paid them full asking price and covered all my own closing expenses, so it's not like I cheated them, either. I don't know whether you're their son or not, Mr. *Mitchell,* but let me just tell you that if you *are* their son, you're a crappy one. They told me about Ken's heart attack and all their medical expenses. Where have you been? In Manhattan? Worrying about making money?"

"You think I don't know that?" he challenged. Wade's eyes flashed with a touch of a temper she'd seen years before. "I'm not proud of it, but I can fix it."

Tori stood up from her seat. "You're just going to have to find another way to soothe your conscience. Send them on a cruise or something, because you aren't going to browbeat me into selling this land. And that's final. Please leave."

Wade stood, bringing his head a hairbreadth away from scraping the top of her camper. He took a step toward her, and his body loomed large and intimidating in such close proximity.

Tori couldn't help the surge of awareness that ran through her body as he came near. Apparently it was far easier to despise him from a distance. It had been a long time since she'd been in the same room as Wade, and she'd certainly never been this close to him, but her body remembered him. With him inches away, looking down at her with a focused, penetrating intensity, her spine wanted to turn to jelly. His warm scent, a familiar mix of spicy cologne and salty skin, swirled around her with every breath she drew into her lungs.

She finally took a step back, pressing herself against the kitchen counter. She didn't like being this close to Wade. It messed with her focus, and that just made her even more irritated. Tori couldn't let him use his size or sexuality to intimidate her.

"This isn't over," he said, pinning her with his dark green eyes before grabbing his coat and walking out into the cold.

Two

Wade remembered Victoria Sullivan as being smart and beautiful. Apparently she was also the most infuriating and stubborn woman he'd ever encountered.

Wade stomped back to his four-wheeler and stood there a moment, letting the cold sink in and douse the aggravating mix of anger and attraction surging through his veins. When he was back in control, he shrugged into his coat, jumped on the ATV and peeled out of her yard in a doughnut as he used to do as a teenager. The back tires sent a sheet of snow flying against the side of her trailer. It was juvenile, but she seemed to bring out the worst in him.

He was fuming as he plowed through the snow. It should be illegal for a woman that gorgeous to have a mouth that irritating. Honestly, once she'd peeled out of her jacket and revealed a snug pair of jeans and a fitted, long-sleeved T-shirt, he'd almost forgotten why he was there. It wasn't until she picked up her shotgun again that he realized he'd followed her inside without her permission.

Victoria had been one of his best and brightest architects. He'd hired her straight out of college when the company he and Alex had started was still small and spending more than it earned. She'd contributed quite a bit to making their first few big projects a success. He'd even considered asking her out to dinner. But then his assistant had come to him with concerns about seeing Victoria at a restaurant looking a little too cozy with one of their potential suppliers. She had been quite vocal about giving the man an upcoming contract, and the implication was clear. He fired her on the spot. Part of him regretted that. And not just because she had knockout curves, flawless skin and long, fiery red hair that made him warm under the collar.

He had wanted to believe her when she said she didn't do it. The thought of her with another man nearly made him crazy. But the logical part of his brain was infuriated by her audacious attempt to influence corporate contracts like that. Sleeping with a potential contractor was just as bad as taking bribes from one. Both compromised a person's objectivity and put the ethics of his company in question.

He would not have it, so he terminated her. He never dreamed the decision would come back to haunt him.

If she were any other woman, he would've asked her to dinner to talk over his offer and kissed her to keep the inflammatory words from flying out of her mouth. Her temper, as spicy as her hair, was a massive turn-on. He had a weakness for redheads.

But she wasn't another woman. She was holding on to seven years of bitterness along with the key to something more important to him than anything else. Protecting his family was his number one priority. Toying with Victoria like a cat with a mouse could cost him dearly. He needed her to sell him this land. He couldn't fail. As much as he'd like to resolve their differences between the sheets, it wasn't the answer in this situation. He doubted it would sway her, and she'd probably shoot him if he tried to kiss her.

"Arrogant and pigheaded," Wade grumbled, turning to steer the four-wheeler down the center aisle of trees toward the entrance. She thought she knew so much. Well, she forgot rich, powerful, ruthless and determined Wade Mitchell came in the same package. He would secure that land and protect his family one way or another.

Wade came to an abrupt stop as an old pickup truck, draped in Christmas lights and garland, pulled in front of him. Piled into the trailer it towed was a crowd of bundled-up people sitting on bales of hay and singing Christmas carols. The driver, Owen, threw a hand up at Wade, then continued back toward the house.

Hayrides, Santa visits, sugar cookies and hot chocolate. Picking out a tree at the Garden of Eden wasn't just a shopping trip. It was an experience. On the weekends in December, the farm was a madhouse. And it had to be. A good portion of their income came from just this one month. Sure, they did other things throughout the year, but Christmas tree farms depended on a good Christmas to stay afloat.

And lately, it hadn't been enough.

Wade blamed himself for that. When the boys grew up and moved away, the Edens had to hire in help. Owen had always worked on the farm, but as each year went by, more staff was added and their expenses went up. Throw in a mountain of hospital bills and competition from increasingly more realistic fake trees, and the Edens were lucky they'd survived this long.

Wade followed the truck to the house and then veered off to park the ATV back under the awning where they kept it. The farm would be closing soon, so he skipped the house and headed around to the tree-processing area. Heart attack be damned, he found his dad out there with a couple of teenage boys. They were leveling, drilling, shaking and net-bagging all the trees selected by the last round of customers.

As though he'd never left, Wade grabbed a tree and put it on the shaker to remove any loose needles. When it was done, Ken laid the tree out to drill. They carried special stands in the gift shop that ensured a perfectly straight tree.

Wade held it still while Ken drilled.

"You haven't lost your touch, kid. Need a job?"

Wade smiled. "I could work for about a week. Then I've got to get back to town."

"That's fine, fine. We'll be closed by then, anyway." Ken lifted the tree and gave it to one of the boys to run through the netter. When he turned back, he gave Wade a big welcome hug. "Good to see you, son."

"Good to see you, too, Dad. Is that the last of the trees for tonight?"

"Yep. With perfect timing, you've shown up just when all the hard work is finished. Come help me haul these trees out to the parking lot and we'll go see your mother."

Wade grasped a tree in each hand and followed his father through the snow to the parking lot where the last few cars waited for their trees. He watched his father carefully for signs of ill health as he hauled around the trees and helped families tie them into trunks and onto roofs. The man wasn't quite sixty yet and had always appeared to be at the peak of health. His brown hair was mostly gray now, but his blue eyes were still bright and alert, and he didn't hesitate in his physical work. Ken had always been a lean man, but a strong man. If nothing else, he looked a little leaner than usual.

"There's nothing wrong with me, so quit looking for it." Ken snatched the last tree from Wade and hauled it down to the pickup truck waiting for it.

Wade followed him, then stood quietly until the truck pulled away. "I wasn't looking for anything."

"Liar. Everyone has been doing it since your mother told Julianne about that damned attack I had. It was no big deal. I'm fine. They gave me a pill to take. End of story. Don't be sitting around waiting for me to drop dead so you can inherit this place."

Both men chuckled, knowing Wade could buy and sell the farm ten times over and had no interest in getting his claws on any inheritance. "You're looking good to me, Dad."

"Yeah." He slapped Wade on the back and started walking toward the gift shop. "Most days I feel okay. I'm slowing down a little. Feeling my age. But that's just reality. The attack threw me for a loop—just came out of the blue. But between the pills and your mother's dogged determination to feed me oatmeal and vegetables, I should be fine. What are you doing up here so early, Wade? You kids don't usually show up until Christmas Eve."

"I had some time in my schedule, so I thought I'd spend it with you guys. Help out. I know I don't visit enough."

"Well, that's a nice lie. Be sure to tell your mother

that. She'll eat it up. All of you boys are in a panic since you found out we sold that land."

"I wouldn't call it a panic."

"Wouldn't you, now? Four out of the five of you kids have been here in the past month, just randomly checking in. I'm sure Xander would've come, too, if congress wasn't in session fighting over the stupid budget."

Wade shrugged. "Well, what do you expect, Dad? You kept your heart attack a secret. You're having financial trouble and you don't tell any of us. You know we all make good money. There was no need to start selling off the farm."

"I didn't sell off the farm. I sold off some useless rocks and dirt that were costing more money than they earned. And yes, you make a good living. I haven't made a good living in quite a few years. One doesn't make up for the other."

"Dad—"

Ken stopped in front of the gift shop, his hand on the doorknob. "I don't want any of your money, Wade. I don't want a dime from any of you kids. The unexpected medical bills just sucked up our savings. The past few years had been lean and we'd cut back on things, including our insurance, to weather the rough patch. Selling off the extra land let us pay off all the bills, buy a new insurance plan and stick some money away. Less land means less taxes and less for me to worry about. Everything will be just fine."

He pushed open the door to the gift store, ending the conversation. Wade had no choice but to let the subject drop and follow him in. They were instantly bombarded with lights and sounds straight from Santa's workshop. Jingling bells chimed from the door; Christmas music played from overhead speakers. A television in the back was showing holiday cartoons on a constant loop near the area where children could write letters to Santa and play with toys while Mommy shopped and Daddy loaded the tree.

Multicolored lights draped from the ceiling. The scent of pine and mulling spices permeated the room. The fireplace crackled on one wall, inviting customers to sit in rocking chairs and drink the hot chocolate Molly provided free.

"Wade!" The tiny and pleasantly plump woman behind the counter came rushing out to wrap her arms around her oldest boy.

He leaned down to hug her as he'd always had to do, accepting the fussing as she straightened his hair and inspected him for signs of stress or fatigue. She always accused him of working too much. She was probably right, but he'd learned his work ethic from them. "Hey, Mama."

"What a surprise to have you here so soon. Is this just a visit or are you here for the holiday?"

"For the duration."

"That's wonderful," she said, her eyes twinkling with happiness and Christmas lights. "But wait." She paused. "I thought Heath told me you were in Jamaica this week."

"Plans changed. I'm here instead."

"He's checking up on us," Ken called from the counter where he was pouring himself a cup of cider.

"I don't care," she called back. "I'll take him however I can get him." Molly hugged him again, then frowned at her son. "I don't have anything prepared for dinner," she said, aghast at the idea. "I wish I'd known you were coming. I was just going to feed your father a sandwich."

"Whole wheat, fat-free turkey, no mayo, no flavor," Ken grumbled.

"Don't worry about feeding me, Mama. I was going to run into Cornwall to meet a couple of the guys at the Wet Hen and grab a few things from the store. I'll get something to eat at the diner when I'm done."

"All right. But I'm going to the store first thing in the morning, and I'll get stocked up on everything I need to feed a household of boys for the holiday!"

Wade smiled. His mother looked absolutely giddy at the idea of slaving over a stove for five hungry men. He recalled times from his youth when he and the other boys were hitting growth spurts all at once. They couldn't get enough food into their stomachs. Hopefully now they would be easier to take care of.

"Why don't you just give me a list and I'll pick it up while I'm out."

"We don't need your money," Ken called from the rocking chair by the fire, though he didn't turn to face them.

Molly frowned at her husband, and Wade could see she was torn. They did need the money, but Ken was being stubborn. "That would be very nice of you, Wade. I'll write up a few things." She returned to the counter and made out a short list. "This should get us through a few days. I'll go into town for a fresh turkey on Monday morning."

"Okay," he said, leaning down to kiss her cheek. "I'll be back soon. Maybe I'll bring home one of those coconut cream pies from Daisy's."

"That would be lovely. Drive safely in the snow."

Wade stepped through the jingling door and headed

out into the newly darkened night in search of pie, a dozen eggs, a sack of potatoes and some information on Victoria Sullivan.

When Tori got into her truck, she had every intention of going to Daisy's to get something to eat. Maybe swing by the store for some quick and easy-to-prepare food to get her through the holidays when the diner was closed. And yet before she could help herself, her truck pulled into the parking lot of the Wet Hen, the local bar.

"Let's face it," she lamented to her dashboard. "I need a drink."

Just one. Just enough to take the edge off the nerves Wade had agitated. And if it helped suppress the attraction that was buzzing through her veins, all the better.

Tori slid from the cab of her truck, slammed the heavy door behind her and slipped through the door of the Wet Hen. The sign outside claimed the bar had been in business since 1897. Truthfully, it looked as if it had. A renovation wouldn't hurt, but she supposed that was part of its charm. The bar was dark, with old, worn wood on the walls, the floors and the tables. The photos on the walls of various local heroes and the sports memorabilia from the high school seemed to be there more to camouflage cracks in the plaster than anything else. The amber lights did little to illuminate the place, but she supposed a bright light would not only ruin the atmosphere but force the local fire department to condemn it.

The place was pretty quiet for six on a Friday. She imagined business would pick up later unless people were tied up in last-minute holiday activities. She made her way to the empty bar and pulled up a stool. It was from her perch that she heard the laughter of a group of men in the back corner. When she turned, Tori quickly amended her plans. She needed two drinks. Especially with that cocky bastard watching her from the back of the bar.

What was Wade doing here? It was a small town, but wasn't there somewhere else he should be? At home with his all-important family, perhaps? But no, he was throwing back a couple with an odd assortment of old and young men from around town. She recognized her lawyer, Randy Miller, and the old bald sheriff from one of the local television advertisements about the dangers of holiday drinking and driving. There were a couple others there she didn't recognize.

And at the moment, every one of them was looking at her.

Had Wade been talking to them about her? The arrogant curl of his smile and the laughter in the eyes of the other men left no doubt. The irritation pressed up Tori's spine until she was sitting bolt upright in her seat.

She wanted to leave. Not just the bar, but the town. Maybe even the state. In an hour she could have the trailer hooked up and ready to go. Part of the beauty of being nomadic was that you could leave whenever things got uncomfortable. That's what her parents had always done. Hung around somewhere until it got boring or awkward and then moved on to someplace else. Tori had always had trouble imagining living in one community her entire life. There was no place to go when things blew up in your face.

But there were also advantages to being settled: longtime friends and neighbors. People you could count on. Stability. Roots. A place to call home and raise a family. After toying with the idea of having that kind of life with Ryan and then having it all collapse around her, Tori had decided she was tired of running. She might not have the life and family she'd dreamed about with Ryan, but she could have it with someone else if she sat still long enough to have a meaningful relationship.

Cornwall spoke to her. This was where her family had come from and this was where she wanted to stay. But if she was going to build her dream home here, she'd better learn how to tough it out. There was no towing off a house. Being the new girl in a small town was hard enough. Lacking in coping skills wasn't going to help the situation.

If Wade thought he could bully her into selling by turning the town against her, he was in for a surprise. She wasn't going to play along with his charade. If he could play dirty, so could she.

"What can I get you?" The bartender had finally made his way over to her end of the bar. He looked like the kind of guy you'd find at a 115-year-old bar named the Wet Hen. Thin, leathery and gray-haired with an ancient, blurry anchor tattooed on his forearm. The tag pinned to his apron said his name was Skippy. She'd never seen anyone less like a Skippy in her life.

"Gin and tonic with lime." Strong and to the point without stooping to shots. She was tempted to just chug a few big gulps of tequila so she'd no longer care about Wade and his cronies. But she couldn't lose control of her inhibitions, either. Lord knew what kind of trouble she'd get into.

Skippy placed a bowl of peanuts and a napkin on the counter for the drink he quickly poured. He looked as though he had a solid fifty years of experience mixing drinks. When the lowball glass plopped down in front of her, she took a large, quick sip. Damned if that wasn't the best gin and tonic she'd ever had.

Go Skippy.

The alcohol surged straight into her veins. She'd been too agitated to eat anything since Wade left, and her empty stomach gladly soaked up the wicked brew. Three sips into her drink, her worries from earlier had dulled into distant concerns that could be drowned out, along with the loud bursts of male laughter coming from the corner. Thank goodness.

It wasn't until she'd finished her drink and half a bowl of peanuts that she bothered to look in their direction again. Wade was still watching her, although this time the amusement on his face was gone. As the other men around the table chatted, he seemed to have narrowed his focus to her. The expression on his face was quite serious. And openly appreciative of whatever he was seeing.

When their gazes met, Tori felt a jolt of electricity that ran down her spine and prickled across her skin like delicate flames licking at her. It was almost as though his look caressed her physically and drew her into him. It was the same feeling she'd had when he touched her today, handing her the honey jar. Sudden. Unexpected. Powerful.

And totally and completely unwanted.

The clunk of a glass on the bar in front of her startled Tori out of Wade's tractor beam. When she turned, she saw a fresh glass, courtesy of Skippy.

"This one's on the oldest Eden boy."

It took Tori a minute to figure out that probably meant Wade. "You mean the dark-headed one in the green shirt with the smug expression on his face?"

Skippy leaned onto the bar and turned toward the men in the back. "Yep."

"I thought his last name was Mitchell."

"It is."

"Then why'd you call him an Eden boy?"

Skippy shrugged. "'Cause that's what he is."

Tori frowned. Wade's family tree seemed to be a touch more complicated than she'd anticipated. "Tell him I don't want it."

Skippy snorted and shook his head. "He's sitting with the mayor, the sheriff, the best lawyer in town and the city councilman who granted my liquor license. Sorry, kiddo, but I'm not getting involved. You'll have to tell him that yourself."

"Fine," Tori said. The drink was making her feel brave anyway. Scooping up the full glass, she slid off the stool a little too fluidly and made her way across the bar to the table of men in the back.

All five of them halted their conversation and turned to look at her when she approached.

"You're welcome, Miss Sullivan," Wade said with a smile that made her stomach flutter and pissed her off at the same time. He was too cocky for his own good.

"Actually, I wasn't coming to thank you. I'm returning it."

"Is something wrong with the drink?" Wade challenged.

"Nothing aside from it being purchased by you." She set it down on the edge of the table in front of him. "No thanks."

A couple of the men chuckled softly and another shifted uncomfortably in his seat. Wade ignored them all, his gaze laser-focused on her. "Oh, come on, now.

Don't be that way. It was a 'Welcome to Cornwall' drink. A taste of some local hospitality."

"I've lived here for two months and only four people have bothered to speak to me the entire time. It's a little late for a warm welcome. Especially coming from the man who's trying to run me out of town."

"That's harsh. You can stay in town. Just not on that particular spot. Maybe Randy here can help you buy a new place." Wade slapped the younger man beside him on the shoulder. "He tells me he handled the sale of my parents' property."

"*My* property," she emphasized. "What else did he tell you, Wade? Are there any loopholes you can use to nullify the sale? Or are you just snooping around town trying to find some dirt on me you can use for blackmail?"

Wade shrugged casually, and Tori could feel her blood nearly boil in her veins with anger. "Not everything is about you, Miss Sullivan. I'm visiting my friends while I'm in town. If they just so happen to have information about you, then great. I like to be well-informed. Especially when going up against a worthy adversary."

"Don't flatter me. You can dig all you want, but you're not going to find any dirt, because I haven't done anything wrong. I'm not selling you my property, Mr. Mitchell. And that's final." Tori spun on her heel and took two big steps away before she heard the sound of muffled snickers behind her and a poorly masked whisper that suggested Wade's skills in the bedroom might improve her attitude.

That was the last straw. Snapping her head around, she caught Wade smirking at her backside as though he agreed with his uncouth companion's assessment.

She returned to their table. "I'm sorry, what was that? I can assure you my attitude was just fine until you started bullying me around. You may live in a world where you always get your way, but it's not going to happen this time. And neither your money nor your penis is going to change that. I'm not interested in either of them."

With that, she picked up her drink, watching as Wade assessed her with curious eyes. He'd had the good sense to shelve the smirk. "On second thought," she said with a sickeningly sweet smile, "I think I will take this drink. You could use a little cooling off." With a flick of her wrist Tori emptied the glass into Wade's lap.

The icy cold drink shocked him upright out of the chair, sending ice cubes scattering across the floor. Tori turned and walked back to the bar, ignoring his stream of profanity muffled by his friends' howls of laughter. She paid her bill, leaving a nice tip for Skippy, and headed for the door.

Curiosity was nagging at her, but she wouldn't allow herself to turn around and see what Wade was doing. She would give anything to see that smug look wiped off his face, and she was pretty sure that would do it. But looking back meant that she cared. She didn't want to give Wade that satisfaction. Instead, she marched out the front door and headed to her truck. She was nearly to the corner of the building when she heard rapid, heavy footsteps coming up behind her.

"What is your problem?" Wade snarled over her shoulder.

As calmly as she could, Tori turned to look at him. Even with a tight jaw and an angry red flush tainting his perfect, aristocratic features, he was the most hand-

some man she'd ever seen in person. And she hated
that that was her first thought when she looked at him.
Those kinds of thoughts weren't helpful when dealing
with the enemy. And that's what he was, despite the
facade he put up to play nice and the way her body reacted when he was close by.

Judging by the snarl that had replaced his cajoling
smile and the giant wet spot sprawled across his pants,
she was pretty sure he was done playing nice. And that
was fine by her. It would be much easier to deal with
Wade when he wasn't trying to be charming. It just
crossed the wires in her brain and made her think unproductive thoughts.

"My problem?" Tori said coolly. "I don't have a
problem. You're the one who needs something, not me."

"And dumping a drink in my lap is the solution?"

Now it was Tori's turn to shrug dismissively, as he
had. "It seemed like a good idea at the time. You all
were having too much fun at my expense. Just because
you have drinks with the mayor doesn't mean you can
bully me."

Wade narrowed his green gaze at her, slowly stepping forward until she found herself backed up against
the crumbling brick wall of the Hen. With one hand
planted on the wall on each side of her, he'd made sure
there was nowhere for her to go. Tori straightened her
spine and looked defiantly at him as he closed in.

"I never had any intention of bullying you, Miss
Sullivan."

Tori tried not to watch the soft curve of his lips as he
spoke to her, but he was so close she had little choice.
She remembered how she'd once fantasized about kissing those lips. Of course, that was before he turned on
her and threw her out of his company on her rear end.

The surge of anger doused the old memories, and her gaze met his.

"What then?" she asked, her voice laced with sarcasm. "Were you going to take your friend's suggestion and seduce me? Certainly you're so masterful in the bedroom that one good romp would change my mind, right?"

Wade moved a fraction of an inch closer to her. For a moment Tori tensed, thinking he might be leaning in to kiss her. She wanted him to, and she didn't. She'd probably thoroughly enjoy it and then slap him when it was over. It was hard to think with him this close. He stopped short of touching his lips to hers. She could feel his warm breath on her skin.

"I've never had a woman offer me real estate after sex, but it wouldn't be the first time one of my lovers felt the need to repay me for a fantastically pleasurable night together."

Just the words *fantastically pleasurable* wrought a hard throb of need. She fought the urge to lean in to him. To discover what it would feel like to have his hard angles pressing into her soft curves. It had been a long time since she'd even let herself think of something like that. Not since things blew up with Ryan. She didn't trust herself to make the right choices, even with the right kind of man.

And this was the absolute wrong man to light up her libido. He was too smooth. Too charming and certain of himself. It didn't matter what he said or did, for every move he made was a strategic one. But that didn't mean her every move couldn't be a tactical one, as well. He already believed she could be manipulated through sex, or he never would've fired her. Let him think he was getting to her. Let him think he was winning.

Tori pressed a gentle hand to his chest. Her lips parted in invitation; a ragged breath of arousal escaped from her lungs. It wasn't hard to play along: she just gave in to her impulses. She could feel his heart racing just as quickly as her own. He was not immune to his own game. They were both playing with fire.

"What makes you think I want you?" she whispered.

Granting her silent wish, he leaned in and pressed himself against her. The warmth of his hard body radiated through his clothing. The salty scent of male skin mingled with pine. Wade let his lips graze, nestling touches light as feathers along her jaw to her earlobe. The sensitive hollow of her neck sizzled with a touch that tempted and teased without giving her what she really wanted: his mouth against her skin and his hands beneath her shirt.

"Oh, you want me," he whispered confidently into her ear. "Of that I'm certain." Pulling away and taking all the night's warmth with him, he met her gaze and smiled widely. "Good night, Miss Sullivan."

She watched him stroll confidently down the sidewalk and disappear around the corner. She waited until the night was silent and still before she let the air out of her lungs. That man had managed to build a fire in her she hadn't expected, especially considering how much she despised him. This was a dangerous game, but if he was trying to seduce her into selling, it would at least be more pleasurable than fighting. Especially when he lost.

A smile of amusement curled her lips. "Oh, you only think you won this round, Wade Mitchell. But the fun is just beginning."

Three

By the time Wade returned to the farm that night, the lights in the big house were all out except for the front porch and the kitchen. His parents had always been early to bed, early to rise, as most farmers were. Thank goodness for the bunkhouse.

The renovated barn referred to as "the bunkhouse" had been where all the boys slept and played as kids. The historic Federal-style house that came with the farm was large, but old in style and design, never renovated to have enough bedrooms and bathrooms to accommodate an ever-changing herd of boys and Julianne all at once. But none of the boys minded the separation.

The bunkhouse had been the perfect boys' retreat, and Julianne spent her fair share of time over there, as well. The entire downstairs was an open living area where they could do their homework, watch television, play video games and Ping-Pong, and roughhouse without breaking anything important. They even had their own mini-kitchen with a refrigerator, microwave and sink. As growing boys they were starving at all hours, and Molly didn't want them running across the yard to the house in the cold and dark.

Upstairs were two huge bedrooms and adjoining baths. The rooms had twin beds and a set of bunk beds to accommodate up to six foster boys at one time. In addition to Wade and his brothers, there had been other children who came but didn't stay long because they went back to their parents or were adopted by relatives. They rarely had an empty bed back then.

These days there were just the four of them, each having outgrown bunk beds. Molly had redecorated after they all moved out, and each room now had two queen-size beds. Typically the kids all arrived back at the farm at the same time: Christmas Eve. The big house hadn't gotten any larger in the past decade, so the boys found themselves back in the bunkhouse.

Since he was the only one there, Wade could stay in the upstairs guest room of the big house. At least until Christmas when the others arrived. But somehow that felt wrong. Instead, he carried Molly's requested groceries inside the big house, put them away and then locked the back door behind him. He grabbed the rest of his things from the hatch of his SUV and rolled his suitcase over to the bunkhouse.

Anticipating his move, Molly had left the porch light on, and on the mini-kitchen counter was a slice of lemon pound cake wrapped in cellophane and a note welcoming him home.

As he read the note he smiled and set the rest of his groceries beside it. He stashed a small case of water, cream cheese, Sumatran coffee beans and a six-pack of his favorite microbrewed dark ale in the fridge. He left the bagels and a bag of pretzels on the counter beside the cake.

God, it was nice to be home.

His loft apartment in Tribeca was nice—it should be, considering what he paid for it. But it didn't feel like home. With its big glass windows and concrete floors, it was a little too modern in design to feel welcoming. It was chic and functional, which is what he thought he liked when he bought it. But it wasn't until he set foot in this old barn with the battered table-tennis table and ancient two-hundred-pound television that he could truly relax.

Things hadn't changed much in the bunkhouse. The futon where he first made out with Anna Chissom was still in the corner. She'd been his first girlfriend, a shy, quiet redhead who kicked off a long string of auburn-haired women in his life. The latest, of course, was giving him the most grief. But he still wished he could pull Victoria down onto the futon and finish what they'd started outside that bar.

He'd done it intending to get under her skin and punish her for dumping that drink on him. Then he found he liked touching her. Teasing her. He enjoyed the flush upon her creamy fair skin. The soft parting of her lips inviting him to kiss her. She responded to him, whether she wanted to or not, exposing her weakness. Now he just had to take advantage of it. There were worse negotiating tactics. Yet she wasn't the only one suffering. He wanted to feel her mouth against his. And not just so she'd sell him her land.

Wade flopped back onto the couch and eyed his watch. It was only nine-thirty. He didn't normally go to bed until well after eleven, especially on the weekends. He was tempted to pull out his laptop and get some work done but was interrupted by the faint melody of his phone.

It was Brody's ringtone—the dramatic pipe-organ melody of the theme to *The Phantom of the Opera*. It was a long-running family joke, considering his computer-genius brother was pretty much living out the plotline as a scarred recluse. But when you had the kind of life that most of the Eden boys had lived, you developed a pretty thick skin and a dark sense of humor to make it through.

"Hey, Brody," Wade answered.

"Wade." His brother's tone was cautious and, as always, serious.

"No," Wade said, cutting off the next question. "I went out to the property to talk to the owner, but there's a…*complication*."

Brody sighed heavily. "I knew this wouldn't be as easy as you seemed to think."

"I said a complication, not a complete failure, Debbie Downer. It's just not going to be open-and-shut. The owner is reluctant to sell."

"Even at double the price?"

"I offered her half a million and she turned me down flat."

Brody groaned on the line. "Why on earth would she turn that down? Half a million dollars is a lot to just push aside."

"Well, it's partially my fault." And technically, it was. He had the feeling Victoria Sullivan might've sold the land if any of his brothers had shown up at her doorstep. But not Wade. Oh, no. She was bound and determined to get back at him for firing her, even though it was her own doing.

"What did you do?" Brody asked in the same sharp tone he'd always used as a child. Whenever one of the other boys lamented about being punished, those were always the first words out of his mouth. Brody was the one who never got into trouble, who never did anything wrong. He was too worried about being punished, thanks to his abusive father. Brody was always happiest sitting at his computer, whether he was playing games or helping Molly upgrade to the latest financial management software. He never got into trouble.

"I didn't *do* anything. She just doesn't like me. She used to work for me years ago."

"Did you sleep with her?"

Wade couldn't help snorting into the phone at his brother's assumption that this had to be a spurned lover. Compared to the lifestyle of his brother, he supposed he appeared to be a bit of a dog when it came to the ladies. "Then or now?" he teased.

"Either."

"No, I've never slept with her." Despite the fact that he would like to. Very much. He eyed the mostly dry spot on the crotch of his pants and smiled. She was a feisty one, for sure. He was certain they'd have a hell of a time in bed. But if she didn't like him enough to conduct a business deal, she probably didn't like him enough to take her clothes off for him.

Well, at least not yet. He'd seen the passion blazing in her pale blue eyes as he'd pinned her against that wall tonight. She wanted him, all right. But she was too stubborn to give in to it.

"I fired her. For cause, I might add. She still seems to be a little perturbed about that."

"I knew we should've sent Xander. No one can say no to him."

Their brother Xander was a Connecticut congress-man. He was smooth, charming, likable and well-spoken. Everything a good politician needed to be. He would be perfect to handle the situation, if he were available. "Well, Xander is busy negotiating the country out of a huge deficit, so you're stuck with me. I can make this happen. I assure you. It just isn't going to get done in a day. She's going to take some convincing."

"What can I do to help it along? Run a background check? See if I can dig up any information on her?"

"That wouldn't hurt, although I doubt you'll come up with anything useful. At least, not anything black-mail worthy. I get the feeling her faux pas at my company was a fluke."

"Maybe there's something in her history you can use to soften her up. It will make me feel like I'm doing something."

Wade could hear the aggravation in his brother's voice. Brody wanted to help, but not much could be done from the supersecure corporate offices of his soft-ware empire in Boston. His brother was brilliant, had built a company that rivaled Google and Facebook, but Brody didn't go out in public. The only time anyone saw him was when he came home for Christmas or Easter. The rest of the time it was just he and his sec-retary, Agnes, on the top floor of his Boston high-rise.

It was a damn shame. If Brody's biological father ever got parole, Wade would make him wish he'd stayed in jail. The kind of bastard who would dump battery acid on his young son's face didn't deserve to see the light of day. Especially not when his son didn't get to see it, either.

"For now, some good intel may be all I need to con-vince her. She doesn't like me, but if I know what buttons to push, maybe I can change her mind. Look into her company for me and some of her recent projects. I'll send you the basic info to get started. I know she's passionate about her work. That might be all it takes. If I'm right, and this is the right property, once I secure it, there won't be any more trouble. If she holds out, maybe you and I can go out in the dark over the holiday and start digging holes."

"Digging holes in the dark?"

"You said you wanted to help," Wade pointed out, only half joking. If the shovels came out, they had big, big problems.

"Don't let it get to that point, Wade. This isn't a missing time capsule we're looking for here. It's a dead man's body. One that we all share some responsibility for putting into the ground. It absolutely can't be found. Do whatever it takes to fix this. It could ruin all our reputations—maybe even our companies. Who wants to do business with someone involved in the death of—"

"Just stop," Wade interrupted. He didn't even want the words spoken aloud.

"This could kill Dad with his heart condition. I don't want another death on my conscience."

Neither did Wade. It would probably do all that and more. And if it didn't kill Ken, Wade was certain he wouldn't be able to bear the look of disappointment on his father's face. He'd spent his whole life trying to be good enough. For his teenage birth mother, who had dumped him on an old relative. For the foster families that had passed him around like a hot potato. For the Edens, who had treated him like their son. He couldn't, wouldn't disappoint Ken and Molly.

He'd already failed fifteen years ago to protect his

brothers and sister as he should have. Wade wouldn't make that same mistake twice.

"I'll handle it," he promised. "One way or another."

"Welcome to the Garden of Eden Tree Farm. I hope we can help you have a very merry Christmas!"

The moment Tori crossed the threshold into the gift shop among the jingling of bells, Molly Eden greeted her from her post behind the counter. Tori had met the older woman once, at closing, but there had been paperwork to sign and not much time for chitchat.

Today she was determined to change that. Wade thought he could sneak around town and get information on her. Well, two could play at that game. And what better source than his mother? He claimed his family was more important than anything, even money. Spending some quality time with them under the guise of Christmas shopping was the perfect way to do a little digging of her own.

"Oh, Miss Sullivan!" Molly came out from behind the counter with a wide smile that was bookended by rosy cheeks. The woman was tiny and round, with gray-blond hair swept up into a neat bun at the back of her head. In about ten more years, once her hair had gone completely white, she'd make the perfect Mrs. Claus. And judging by her surroundings, Tori was pretty sure that was the plan all along.

"Please call me Tori."

"Only if you call me Molly, dear. We're neighbors, after all." Molly embraced her as though they were lifelong friends instead of acquaintances through real estate.

Tori smiled. She couldn't help it. The woman was

just so damn sweet. How was it that she could raise a sneaky corporate weasel like Wade? "That we are."

She noticed that nothing in the woman's tone or expression conveyed any hint of concern about the fact that Tori lived on her old land. The same was true when they'd met at closing. Neither she nor Ken had seemed bothered at all by it. In fact, Ken had appeared a little relieved. She remembered Ken had commented that they were getting to an age where nearly three hundred acres was a lot of land to deal with. Tori's piece was too rocky and sloped to grow trees. The other two larger plots were the same. No great loss there.

So why did it bother Wade so much that they'd sold it? It made Tori wonder if his parents even knew what he was up to. The burning, childish urge to tattle on him swirled in her gut. It would be so easy. Even a millionaire CEO could be brought down by the wrath of his mama.

But somehow that didn't seem like fighting fair. They hadn't taken the gloves off yet. She'd reserve that tactic until it was absolutely necessary. In the meantime, there wasn't any harm in being neighborly. She wasn't very good at it, since her neighbors typically changed out every few weeks, but she was willing to give it a try.

"So what brings you by today? Do you need a tree?"

"Oh, no," Tori said. "I don't have room for one in my little trailer. When the house is finished, I'll get one for sure. But for now I thought I might pick up one of the lovely fresh pine wreaths you put together. When I was down at Daisy's the other night, the waitress Rose was bragging on your artistic skills."

Molly was beaming with pride as she led Tori over to the display of wreaths. "Rose is such a sweetheart.

She used to date my Xander when they were in high school. I hate that it didn't work out."

They stopped in front of a stone wall covered in about ten different wreaths. There was a variety of sizes, all with decorations of different styles. Tori wasn't really in the market for a wreath, but she would buy one. If she didn't, she'd probably buy a package or two of the homemade fudge by the register, and she certainly didn't need that.

She picked the first one that really caught her eye. "That blue-and-silver wreath is gorgeous. I think I'll take that one."

"That's one of my favorites, too. Let me get the hook to get it down."

Molly headed off across the store, pausing only when the jingling of bells signaled someone else had come in. "Oh, Wade, perfect timing. Could you get that blue wreath down for me?"

Tori snapped her head around to see Wade shaking the snow off his boots on the entryway rug. Today he was wearing a deep red cashmere sweater with a white collared shirt beneath it. It made his shoulders look impossibly wide and strong. After being so close to him last night, she found it wasn't hard to imagine being wrapped in his arms. And being pressed against his chest... Tori shook her head to chase away the unproductive thoughts.

"Sure, Mama," he said without turning her way.

"And I want you to meet Tori Sullivan," Molly continued. "She's the one who bought that little piece of land near the ridge."

At that, Wade stiffened and turned in her direction. He frowned for only a moment, wiping the expression from his face before his mother could see it. He followed her over to the wreath display and, without speaking, lowered the blue-and-silver wreath into his mother's arms.

"Tori, this is my oldest son, Wade. He's in real estate in New York. Perhaps you two run in the same circles. Wade, Tori is an architect. She bought one of our lots, and she's designing a beautiful house to build up there."

"You flatter me," she said, avoiding Wade's gaze until she had to greet him. When she did, there was a polite blankness in his eyes. He was obviously going to pretend they had never met before. She was willing to play along with that for now. "It's nice to meet you, Wade." She held out her hand to him.

"And you, Tori," he said very formally, while managing to emphasize the pronunciation of her first name. It was the first time he'd called her that since he'd shown up at her trailer. Actually, it was the first time he'd ever called her "Tori." When she'd worked for his company, she'd gone by Victoria. She couldn't help but watch his lips as he said her name. There was something oddly seductive about the way his mouth moved that just wasn't there when he called her Miss Sullivan.

When he finally reached out and shook her hand, Tori realized a second too late that touching him was probably a bad idea. She was right. The minute his hand encompassed hers, it was as though she had dipped it into a warm bath. The heat of his soft touch engulfed her, sending a delicious surge of need up her arm that tightened her chest and made it hard to breathe. She found she couldn't pull away from him.

Her body was betraying her, and for what? A chaste, polite handshake?

But then she looked into his dark green eyes and realized it was more than that. He, too, felt the current of desire that traveled through their skin-on-skin contact. Unlike last night, when Wade was prepared and in control of the seduction, this seemed to catch him off guard. For just a brief moment the animosity and arrogance was stripped away, leaving him only with the expression of pure, unadulterated desire. He was fighting the urge to devour her, then and there.

His gaze was so penetrating, it felt like a caress. When his thumb gently stroked the back of her hand, her heart started racing, her breath quick in her throat the way it had been the night before when she thought he might kiss her. The feeling was intense. Too intense for a Christmas store with his mother only a few feet away.

Tori jerked away suddenly, hoping Molly didn't notice the invisible sparks as she rubbed her palm on her jeans to deaden the lingering sensation from his touch. Wade's eyes didn't stray from hers for a few moments, intently searching her as though he were looking into her soul. He turned away only when Molly spoke.

"Tori, I'm going to get this wreath boxed up for you. Do you have a hook to hang it?"

"No," she admitted, sounding oddly out of breath for someone standing still. "Pick whatever one you think will look the nicest with it, and I'll take that, too."

Molly grinned and dashed off to the other side of the store, leaving Wade and Tori alone.

"What are you doing here?" he asked, his tone unquestionably accusatory, yet low enough for his mother not to hear them.

Tori crossed her arms under her breasts, burying her still-burning hand. "Shopping, obviously."

This time, when his green gaze raked over her, there

was no heat behind it. Just irritation and suspicion. "Did you come here to get back at me for last night?"

"Get back at you for what? You claimed you were just hanging out with some friends. Do you think I came here to tattle on you to your mama?"

"No," he said, although the deep lines of the wary expression on his face gave away his lie.

Tori cracked a wicked grin, knowing she'd easily discovered an Achilles' heel. Of course, any son of a decent family had a soft spot where his mother was concerned. Even the pushy, arrogant sons. She opted to rub it in by parroting the line he'd used on her last night. "I'm here buying some Christmas decorations. If your mama just happens to supply me with some information about you, then great. I like to be well-informed. Especially when going up against a worthy adversary."

"Touché," he said drily before casting a quick glance over his shoulder to see where Molly was.

"I take it Ken and Molly don't know what you're trying to do to me?"

His head snapped back to look at her. *"Do to you?"* he whispered with a touch of incredulity in his voice. "Offering to pay you four times your property value is hardly twisting your arm. But no, they don't know about it, and I'd like to keep it that way. They don't need any more stress."

"If they don't care, why are you so determined to get it back? I don't understand."

A barrier went up inside Wade. Tori could almost feel the steel walls slamming into place. She'd obviously trodden into dangerous territory with him.

"I don't have to explain to you why this land is important to me. All you need to know is that I intend to get it back one way or another."

"So you seem to think."

Tori watched as Wade's hands curled into controlled fists at his side. She couldn't tell whether he wanted to kiss her senseless or bludgeon her with a nearby reindeer statue. But he couldn't do any of those things. Not with Molly nearby. Tori had no doubt he'd give her a piece of his mind the minute he could. She was kind of looking forward to it.

"Wade?" His mother's voice called over the cheerful carols playing in the store.

They both turned to look at his mother, and Tori noticed a curious expression on Molly's face. She seemed...intrigued by their quiet discussion. Tori hoped she hadn't mistaken their subdued animosity for real attraction. Tori wouldn't put it past her to try to fix them up. Yes, there was a current running beneath the surface, but it was pointless to consider what that meant. Fortunately, Wade's living in New York would easily put a damper on anything Molly tried to start up.

"Coming," Wade said before he shot Tori a heated warning glance and turned away. She watched him talk to Molly for a minute, then nod and walk out of the store without another word to her.

Tori let out a deep breath and realized she'd been holding it long enough for her lungs to start burning. Her whole body was tense from bickering with him and—if she was honest with herself—anxious with the need he built inside her with a simple touch. It was an extremely confusing combination.

"Your package is ready, dear."

Tori returned to the counter. "Thank you. I'm sure it will look great. The silver and blue against the shiny aluminum will be perfect."

"It will," she agreed. "What are you doing for Christmas? Do you have any family nearby?"

Tori shook her head. "No. My parents travel a lot. The last time they called, they were in Oregon. I'll probably call and check in with them Christmas Day, but I haven't spent an actual holiday with them in years."

"What about any brothers and sisters? Aunts? Cousins?"

"I'm an only child. And my family moved so much that we never really connected with our extended family."

"Hmph," Molly said thoughtfully, although Tori wasn't exactly sure what that meant. "Would you like to join me by the fireplace for some hot mulled cider?"

"I don't want to take up your time."

"Posh! The store is empty. Business won't pick up until later today, and then just with last-minute folk in a rush. Come on, I'll fix you a cup. I've also got some snickerdoodles I took out of the oven right before you came in."

Unable to turn down the Christmas pied piper, she followed Molly over to the refreshment stand, then to the rocking chairs in front of the fireplace.

"You guys really have a lovely place here. It's like a child's Christmas fantasy."

"Thank you. That's really what we were going for—a treasured holiday tradition as opposed to just a shopping trip. Ken and I have always loved children. We'd hoped to have at least five or six." Tori watched Molly gently finger the rim of her paper cup as she spoke. "When that didn't work out, of course, we started taking in foster kids. Wade was the first child we took in."

"Oh," Tori said, the pieces of her conversations with Wade and the bartender finally clicking into place. That was why he had a different last name from the people he considered his parents. He obviously adored Molly as though she were his biological mother. Perhaps not all of his story was meant to play on her emotions. It was possible he did want to preserve the land that had been a special home for him.

Did that change how she felt about selling her property? No. But it did change a little of how she felt about him.

"I didn't realize Wade was a foster child."

"Yes. Julianne is the only child nature blessed us with. The rest came to us through the Litchfield County Social Services office. We had so many over the years, but Wade, Brody, Xander and Heath were the ones who really became a part of our family. It gave us a lot of joy to give a home to children who really needed one. We'd hoped that one day we would be able to turn the farm over to one of them, but that probably won't happen. We raised them to dream big, and they did. Unfortunately, none of them dreamed of being a Christmas tree farmer."

Tori took a bite of one of the warm cookies and nearly moaned with pleasure. The cinnamon, sugar and butter were a divine combination. She'd honestly never had a cookie this good before. "Oh, Molly, this cookie is wonderful. I couldn't have expected anything less with everything you have here. I never had a Christmas tree growing up, but I always imagined buying one at a place like this."

"You've never had a Christmas tree?" Molly looked appalled.

"No. My family liked to travel. My mom homeschooled me so we could move from one town to the next every few weeks. The camper wasn't much bigger than the one I have now, so no real room for a tree. Sometimes, on Christmas morning, my parents would get up really early and decorate one of the nearby trees in the RV park where we were staying."

"Christmas in a camper." Tori could see the wheels turning in Molly's head. "Then I suppose a huge turkey with all the trimmings and homemade pies were out of the question."

Tori chuckled. "Not once in my life have I ever had that. My parents are hippies, really, so they were more into tofu and organic vegetables when I was young. And, yes, even if she'd wanted to cook a turkey, my mom didn't have the room or the equipment. Sometimes we'd eat at a Cracker Barrel when my dad got nostalgic for home-cooked food."

At that, Molly paled beside her. The rosy cheeks had vanished as though Tori had just told her there was no Santa Claus. "You're coming over to our place Monday night for Christmas Eve dinner."

Tori's eyes widened in surprise. "Oh, no," she insisted. Wade would think she'd deliberately done this. He'd make her miserable, glaring accusingly at her across the table all night. "I couldn't possibly intrude on your family dinner."

"Nonsense. Come up to the big house Monday night around five. We'll eat about six, but I want you to get there in time to meet everyone."

"Everyone?" What had Tori gotten herself into?

"It's just me and Ken and the kids. You'll get to meet my other boys. Brody will come up from Boston. He runs a software company. Xander is a congressman, so he's flying back from D.C. Heath, my youngest, will be up from Manhattan. He owns an advertising agency. And my daughter, Julianne, will be home from Long Island. She has a sculpting studio and art gallery in the Hamptons. I'm so excited. I only get them all together once a year. Christmas is a big deal for our family."

Holy crap. Molly made them sound wonderful, but Tori wondered if she wasn't wandering into a trap. How many of them knew about Wade's plans? Would she have his four siblings staring her down, as well? Tori didn't know if she could refuse three powerful CEOs and a congressman if they ganged up on her. She couldn't help imagining herself being slipped a roofie in her eggnog, waking up hog-tied in the basement and being forced to sign over her property.

"Really, thank you, but I already have plans." It wasn't technically a lie. She had planned to eat chicken soup and peanut butter and jelly sandwiches while watching old Christmas movies on DVD. Not good plans, but plans. Hopefully it was enough to appease the older woman.

Molly arched an elegant eyebrow at her. "I have seen your camper, dear. It's really lovely, but I can't imagine you putting together much more than a peanut butter sandwich and a can of soup in there."

Tori smiled. "How did you know what I was having?"

"Oh, Lordy," Molly wailed, dramatically getting up from her chair. "You're coming over for dinner, and that's final."

Tori trailed behind her, tossing her cup and napkin into the trash. She had to admit the idea of some real, home-cooked holiday food was tempting. But she would pay for it later. Wade would see to that. She could see that he got his stubbornness from his mother. The determined glint in Molly's light green eyes left no room for negotiation. Surely Wade would understand his mother was a force of nature.

"Can I bring anything?" Tori had no clue what she could possibly contribute, but her mother had raised her to at least be polite enough to offer.

Molly tried to hide her smile behind her hand and then shook her head. "Not at all. I'll have everything we need. Just bring your darling self, and we'll be waiting for you."

Tori nodded and walked to the cash register to pay for her wreath. She had no doubt Wade would be waiting for her Monday night. Armed and ready for battle.

Four

Tori couldn't make herself go inside the Edens' house. She felt stupid. It was the most unintimidating place she'd ever seen. The old white two-story home was lit with clear icicle lights, and each shutter-framed window had a wreath and candle gracing it. The two short columns that flanked the three stairs leading up to the front door were wrapped with garland and more lights. She could hear Christmas music and laughter from inside. Golden light shone through the downstairs windows and onto the snow.

It was beautiful. Welcoming. The kind of house you wanted to go caroling to because you knew the owners would give you hot cocoa and cookies.

But there was no walking up the steps. Instead, she stood there freezing, clutching the potted poinsettia she'd brought as a hostess gift.

This was a mistake. She just knew it. Tori had spent

the past few hours pacing in her Airstream, trying to think of a way to get out of coming tonight. And when she wasn't pacing, she was looking around at her empty trailer, considering whether she really preferred to watch sentimental old black-and-white Christmas movies and feast alone on peanut butter and chicken soup.

It was Christmas Eve, a day of family and celebration and community. Unfortunately, she wasn't quick to make friends, and small towns were notoriously hard to crack. The only people she knew in Cornwall were her real-estate lawyer, who was apparently best buddies with her enemy; Rose, the waitress at Daisy's diner; and Wade and Molly. That made for a fairly unmerry Christmas this year if she turned down this invitation.

She just couldn't have two miserable Christmases in a row. Last year she'd hoped to spend it with her boyfriend, Ryan. They both traveled so much with their work, but it had seemed that meeting for the holidays in Colorado would be possible. Instead, he'd canceled at the last second, leaving her with a whopping bill for a winter bungalow for one.

Later she discovered he'd never had any intention of coming. He was married with three kids. Ryan was going to be home with his family no matter what he told her. Dating Tori had been perfect for him because she was always moving around and never pressuring him for more. Their relationship was sustained by phone calls, emails and long weekends together. When she'd mentioned moving permanently to Connecticut, only a few hours from his home near Boston, he panicked and broke it off. Finding out about his whole other life had been just the icing on that miserable cake.

He hadn't been the first womanizer to steal her heart and probably wouldn't be the last. She just had a soft spot for smooth, seductive liars. She confused their calculated moves for cultivated charm, but whatever the label, the relationships didn't end well. Slick and likable, they seduced you with words to get what they wanted, then they walked away, uncaring of the shambles they left behind.

Unfortunately, Wade was one of those men, and despite her better judgment, she could feel the attraction building inside her. She wanted him, even as she plotted and planned to make him suffer for the way he'd treated her. She simply couldn't get her brain and her body on the same page. Would having dinner with his family at Christmas make the situation better or worse?

She supposed that all depended on how he reacted to her being there. Perhaps the best way to make him suffer would be to have a good time tonight. Not let him get to her, by rousing either her anger or her desire for him. Having an excellent meal with the enemy was far better than a subpar meal feeling virtuous and lonely.

"I will have a good time," she said out loud, her breath creating a soft cloud of fog in the cold.

"Of course you will. But if you keep standing out here, you're going to get frostbite."

Tori whipped her head around and saw a man standing in the snow a few feet away from her with an armful of firewood. He looked as if he was in his late twenties, tall and strongly built, with short, light brown hair and a wide disarming smile. Her heart was still racing with surprise when she shook her head and laughed. "You scared the daylights out of me."

"Sorry," he said, although his mischievous expression did not lead her to believe it. "You must be Miss Sullivan."

"Tori, yes," she said, shifting the plant in her arms

so she could reach out to shake his hand. "Which one are you?"

"Heath. I'm the baby, if that helps."

The tall muscular man in front of her hardly qualified as a baby. He held the heavy logs in one arm to shake her hand as though they were made of Styrofoam.

Then a thought struck her. Heath knew who she was and was expecting her. Did Wade know she was coming? "Did your mother tell you I was coming to dinner?"

"She told me when I was peeling potatoes on KP."

"Does Wade know?"

"Nope," Heath said with a wicked gleam of pleasure in his eyes. "What's the fun in that?"

Tori's lips twisted in concern. She wanted to see the expression of surprise and irritation on Wade's face when she walked in, unannounced, to his family Christmas party. Apparently so did Heath. But it still felt like a bit of a trap. "Am I walking into the lion's den here?"

Heath shrugged. "Eh, they're fun lions. They'll play with you before they eat you. Come on, let's go in. I'm freezing out here, and the sooner we get in there, the sooner I get pie."

There was no avoiding it now, despite Heath's assurance that she would be eaten. Hopefully she could get some of this famous pie first. Tori let the youngest Eden boy usher her up the stairs, and he held the door open.

"Look what I found outside!" he announced.

Tori had barely recovered from the sudden rush of warmth and light when she was struck with five sets of eyes. She clutched the plant tightly in her hands and tried to gather some holiday cheer in her expression. It probably ended up coming out a little pained.

Molly and a younger woman who looked very much like her looked up from their napkin folding at the large dining room table. Standing in the living room talking were Ken and another of the boys. This one looked vaguely familiar and a bit like Heath, actually. Another, younger man watched her from his crouch in front of the fireplace. Their expressions varied. Curiosity, cheer, surprise and even a touch of anxiety from the one tending to the fire.

But Wade was nowhere in sight.

"Oh, Tori, you came," Molly said, rounding the dining room table to greet her.

"She was just standing in the snow. What did you tell her about us, Ma?" Heath broke away from Tori's side to carry the wood over to the brother by the fireplace.

"You hush," Molly chided and accepted the poinsettia Tori offered. "This is beautiful. Thank you. I told you that you didn't need to bring anything, dear."

"You told me I didn't need to bring any food," Tori corrected with a smile for her warm welcome.

"You're very sweet. Merry Christmas to you." Molly leaned in to give her a big hug. "Ken," she said as she pulled away, "could you introduce her to everyone while I find a place for this and check on the turkey?"

"Sure thing." The tall, lean frame of Ken Eden ambled toward her, a friendly smile on his face. "Hey there, Miss Sullivan. Merry Christmas."

"Merry Christmas to you, too. And call me Tori, please."

Ken nodded. "Now, you met Heath. He's the youngest and most troublesome of the group."

"I heard that!" a voice shouted from the general direction of the fireplace.

"He also has excellent hearing. This is Xander."

"Xander Langston," Tori said, reaching out to shake the man's hand. Molly had mentioned one of her sons was a politician, but Tori didn't connect the pieces until she saw the man she recognized from television news and advertisements. She'd had no idea Xander Langston was also one of the "Eden boys" until she saw him standing by the couch.

Xander smiled, greeting her with a polished finesse that practicing politics must have perfected. "Welcome, Tori. Sounds like you've heard my name before. Are you a registered voter?" he asked with a touch of humor in his light hazel eyes that let her know he was trying to be funny.

"Not here. My previous residence was a PO box in Philadelphia, but I'll be changing that."

"Excellent. I hope spending time with my family doesn't negatively influence your vote."

"Stop campaigning, Xander." The young woman from the dining room came over, shoving the congressman aside with her shoulder. "Sorry, he has trouble turning it off. I'm Julianne."

"This is my baby girl," Ken said, his blue eyes brightening at the sight of his daughter. "She's the most talented artist you'll ever meet."

"Daddy," she chided in a tone very much like her mother's. "I'm glad you could join us tonight, Tori. We need some more estrogen in this house."

Tori shook her hand. The Edens' only daughter was quite beautiful and looked very much like she imagined Molly had appeared when she was younger. She had long golden-blond hair, light green eyes and a smile that lit up the room. A person's eyes just naturally went to her.

"Brody, quit playing with the fireplace and come meet our guest."

The last of the brothers put down the fireplace poker and made his way over. There was a reluctance in his movements that made Tori wonder if this brother was a part of Wade's plot. He'd made a point of mentioning that all of the children wanted the land back. The others didn't seem to look at her or treat her differently than any other dinner guest.

Then she saw it. As he stepped into the shimmering light of the Christmas tree, the previously darkened side of his face was illuminated. Tori sucked in a surprised breath and stiffened her whole body to keep from reacting inappropriately. Almost the entire left side of Brody's face was horribly scarred; the skin puckered and twisted into a horrible mask. She couldn't even imagine what kind of injury would leave a mark like that.

She noticed that Brody had deliberately hesitated at the edge of the group, almost giving her time to react and process everything before he greeted her. He'd apparently lived with this, and people's reactions, for quite some time. She felt the sudden urge to put him at ease. As quickly as she could, Tori made eye contact and smiled. "It's nice to meet you, Brody."

He reached out and shook her hand, nodding gently to himself. "Nice of you to come," he said, the corners of his mouth curving up in subdued welcome. The unmarred side of his face was quite handsome. She could tell that if he really, truly smiled, it would be very charming. He had beautiful dark blue eyes with thick coal-black lashes that his injury hadn't touched. His gaze was initially wary, perhaps anxious at meeting someone new, but the smile eventually made its way into his sapphire depths.

Julianne frowned, looking around the living room. "Where's Wade?"

"Bringing in the last of the Christmas presents from Brody's car. How exactly did I get saddled with this job on my own? What are all of you doin—"

Wade stopped in front of the Christmas tree, his arms overflowing with brightly wrapped packages. His gaze zeroed in on Tori in the crowd of his family members. Her hair must have made her stand out. For a moment, a confused mix of emotions played across his eyes. There was a flash of anger, irritation, concern, surprise… Then his gaze flicked over to his father, and Wade's jaw tightened to hold in whatever words Tori's sudden appearance brought to his mind.

"Wade, have you met our new neighbor?" Ken seemed oblivious to his son's consternation.

"Yes, I have." Wade lowered the presents to the floor, leaving them beside the small mountain of gifts that was already arranged there. He dusted his hands off on his jeans and pushed the sleeves of his hunter-green sweater up the strong bulge of his muscled forearms. He took a deep breath, cast a few meaningful glances to his siblings and walked over to the group. "Mama introduced us in the shop a couple days ago. I didn't realize you were coming to dinner tonight." Wade speared her with a sharp, accusing gaze.

Tori straightened and put on a polite smile. He was unhappy about her being here. Good. He shouldn't be the only one who got to run around town with a smug grin on his face. "Yes, Molly insisted I come tonight so I wouldn't spend Christmas alone. She's very sweet."

"And stubborn," Heath added with a grin.

"Glad you could join us tonight," Ken said, with a reassuring hand to her shoulder. "Dinner should be ready soon."

From there, the group seemed to disperse. Julianne and Ken disappeared into the kitchen to help Molly. Brody and Heath went back to building the world's greatest fire. Xander made noises about presents in his car and slipped out the back door where Wade had just come in. It left Tori and Wade alone in the entryway, surrounded by twinkling lights and Bing Crosby crooning in the background.

Wade watched her intensely for a moment, letting the pressure of his anger out while no one was watching. His face had grown a bit red from the strain of holding it in for so long. He quickly threw a glance over his shoulder for witnesses before he spoke. "May I take your coat?" The words were stilted. Formal. As they'd been Saturday in the gift shop.

Nodding, Tori stuffed her gloves into her pockets and slipped out of her jacket. Wade took it from her and walked a few feet to the closet. She watched him slip the coat onto a hanger, meticulously straightening it as he spoke. "What the hell do you think you're doing?" His voice was extremely low, almost a hiss.

"Having Christmas dinner," Tori retorted. "Your mother invited me, and there was no telling the woman no."

Wade turned toward her, his brow furrowed. He was still irritated, but some of the red blotches were fading from his neck. He had to know there was no arguing with Molly Eden. She was a force of nature. "You could've had the decency to fake the swine flu and cancel."

Tori crossed her arms over her chest. "It's Christmas

Eve. So sue me if I'd rather spend it with other people than sit alone in my trailer. It was a nice invitation, and I accepted it. You can stand there and believe it's part of my supersecret plan to undermine your dastardly plot. And maybe it is. But there's nothing you can do about it except smile and eat some turkey, unless you want to make a scene and ruin your mother's holiday."

Wade thrust her coat into the closet and shut the door as forcefully as he could without audibly slamming it. He turned to her with venom in his dark eyes. "I told you my family is the most important thing in the world to me. It's the reason I'm willing to pay you more than anyone in their right mind would pay for that land. To preserve my family. You can come here and have dinner. But you'd damn well better know that I won't sit back and let you toy with any of them."

"I'm not out to manipulate people like you are, Wade. I have no intention of doing anything to your family."

"You'd better hope you're right."

"Or what?" Tori challenged.

Wade opened his mouth to answer, but his gaze moved over her shoulder to someone behind her. His defensive posture melted away, his expression softening.

Then Tori heard Heath's amusement-laced voice behind her. "Hey, you guys are standing under the mistletoe."

"Mistletoe?" Molly came running from the kitchen, a gleam of excitement in her eyes.

Wade and Tori both looked above their heads and back at each other with a touch of dismay. Dangling from the ceiling was a small sprig of green leaves tied with a festive red ribbon. What the hell was mistletoe doing in the house? Everyone here was related. If not by blood, by circumstance. His mother never hung mistletoe....

Then it hit him. She'd invited Tori to dinner. She'd hung mistletoe. Molly was plotting. The woman had five children in their late twenties or early thirties and not the slightest forecast of weddings and grandbabies in her future. She must have gotten it in her head that Tori would be perfect for one of her boys. Maybe even him. What was she thinking?

By now, the entire family had piled back into the living room to watch.

"Mama," Wade complained. "Why did you hang this stuff? It's silly."

"It's tradition," Molly countered. "This is the first year I've been able to hang it, so you bet your sweet bippy you're going to play along and make me happy."

Wade swallowed the lump in his throat and turned from his family to look at Tori. She looked even more anxious than he felt. She was stiff, her light blue eyes wide with shock from the unexpected declaration. Her cheeks were slightly flushed. He didn't know if it was from their argument or the embarrassment of kissing him like this.

Two seconds earlier they'd been fighting, and now he had to kiss her in front of his entire family. Several times over the past few days he'd fantasized about doing just that. Running his hands through the silken fire of her hair. Halting the flow of poisonous words from her mouth by kissing her into silence.

But not now. Not like this. Not in front of everyone.

"If you don't do it, I will," Heath offered from the

back. Julianne threw an irritated elbow into his ribs, doubling him over. "Ow, Jules!"

That made Wade frown. He sure as hell wouldn't let Heath anywhere near Tori or the mistletoe. He'd punch his brother in the jaw for even thinking about kissing Tori.

He'd worry about what that meant later.

"Just hurry up and get it over with."

Tori's voice distracted him from his brother's taunt. He frowned at the redhead. Even though the sensible thing to do would be to give her a quick peck and move on, he didn't like her attitude. Never in his life had a woman asked him to "hurry up and get it over with." It made him want to pull her into his arms and kiss her breathless. He wanted her to eat her words.

But doing that in front of his family was dangerous. Brody would worry that he'd let sex distract him from their goal. Molly would start knitting booties. He needed to just kiss her so they could have dinner and send Tori on her way.

"Kiss her!" someone shouted. He wasn't sure who.

Wade took a step forward, Tori's whole body tensing as he did. Leaning in to her, he didn't hesitate to bring his lips to hers. He had every intention of giving her the kind of kiss appropriate for a stranger caught in this awkward ritual. But the moment his skin touched hers, it was just like before. The handshake in the gift shop had nearly thrown him for a loop. Touching her so innocently had sent his blood boiling, and he hadn't been able to make himself pull away.

Just like now.

Tori's mouth was soft and more welcoming than he'd expected. There was no tight-lipped resignation. Instead, she leaned in to him just slightly, tasting like the honey she'd put in his tea a few days earlier. The gesture was enough to coax him into closing his eyes and deepening the kiss. His right hand slipped up to caress her cheek.

The surge of desire that ran through his body urged him forward, keeping him from pulling back the way his brain knew he needed to. In the back of his mind he registered that Tori wasn't pulling away, either. There was something stronger than both of them holding them in place. A tingle of electricity danced across the palm of his hand where he touched her. He wanted to wrap his arms around her. He wanted to forget about their circumstances and press his body against hers.

A loud wolf whistle from one of his brothers startled both of them out of it. As if receiving an unexpected slap, Wade jerked back. Tori did the same. He looked at her, a little startled by his reaction to her. The intensity had completely caught him off guard. Judging by the wide-eyed expression on Tori's face, she was equally confused by what had just happened.

Glancing behind her, he saw that his whole family stood with mixed expressions on their faces. A few were surprised, Brody was irritated, Heath was amused. Only his mother was grinning, a smug satisfaction in her eyes. Wade could tell she was picking out the perfect color of pastel yarn at that very moment.

"Well," Ken said, breaking the awkward silence. "I think it's time to carve this bird. Everyone finish up and make your drinks."

The family scattered again, Molly reluctantly returning to her duties and leaving Wade and Tori alone. He looked back to her, and his chest suddenly felt tight and uncomfortable. The white collared shirt under his sweater was choking him. He was unpleasantly warm, despite being on the opposite side of the room from the fireplace.

Maybe it had nothing to do with his clothes. It was her. She looked more beautiful than she ever had. Her pale skin was flushed a rosy pink. Her lips were moist and slightly parted. The light blue of her eyes seemed darker around the edges than before. Maybe it was the dark blue of her scoop-neck sweater that drew out the color. It highlighted the long column of her neck and the delicate line of her collarbones. Between them, a small cameo hung on a gold chain. It was the ivory silhouette of a woman set against a blue background that reminded him of his mother's Wedgwood.

Wade wanted to sweep the necklace aside and plant kisses in the hollow of her throat. He wanted to know how her skin would taste and smell. He sucked in a deep breath to draw in her scent. It was a smoky mix of sweet flowers, like honeysuckle, and the herbal undertone of burning incense. It was surprisingly seductive.

"What was that?" Tori's voice was small and without the biting tone she normally hurled at him.

"Just a kiss," he answered, dismissing the powerful feeling that had set fire running through his veins when they touched. He wasn't ready to let her know how it had affected him. How she affected him. That would put him at a distinct disadvantage in their negotiations.

Her blue eyes searched his face for a moment before she sighed and looked away. There was a touch of disappointment in her expression as though she'd expected him to acknowledge it was more than that. She nodded softly and took a step away from him. "I'm going to wash my hands before dinner."

Wade pointed out the small half bath beneath the stairs and watched her walk away. The sweater was enticing, but more so were the charcoal-gray skirt and knee-high leather boots she wore with it. There was a sway to her hips when she walked that was deliciously outlined by the fit of the skirt, and the slit in the back offered him a momentary flash of thigh with each step. It made him wish the bathroom were farther away so he could continue to watch her walk.

Brody stepped into the path of his view just as she pulled the door closed behind her. A frown lined his brother's face as he thrust a mug of mulled cider into Wade's hand. "Here. There's no whiskey in it. I figured you were being dumb enough without alcohol."

Wade scowled at his brother but accepted the drink. "You worry too much. It's all part of my plan," he lied, hoping it sounded like forethought on his part. "I'm softening her up. Then, when you dig up some good information on her I can use, she'll be putty in my hands."

Heath came past them to put his own coat into the closet. "Hey, Wade, I thought you were supposed to be buying Tori's land, not checking her for tonsillitis."

"Both of you just cool it. I know what I'm doing."

Brody's dark blue gaze narrowed at him. Wade often wondered if his brother's personality would be different if he had been born into better circumstances. Would he be less serious? More open to life?

"Try not to scowl at her, Brody. Make her feel welcome, more at ease. It will help. You said you wanted to do something. Here's your chance."

Brody sighed. "I know. I just wasn't prepared to see her walk in. I wish Mama had told me she was coming. She knows I don't like those kinds of surprises."

Wade nodded. "Neither do I." He knew his brother didn't like to meet new people. It was a painful ritual he had to repeat every time someone came face-to-face with him for the first time. "How did she do?"

"Better than most. She didn't run screaming or anything. Although, I need to tell Julianne not to sit her across from me at the table. I'm sure it wouldn't help her appetite to look at me the whole time."

Wade sighed and took a sip of his cider. "Stop it. No self-flagellation during the holidays. Would you rather she sits across from me?"

"Hmm," Brody said thoughtfully. "You two might end up playing footsie at this rate. Maybe across from Xander or Heath."

"Dinner is ready," Molly announced from the entryway to the kitchen. "Is everyone ready?"

The bathroom door opened and Tori came out much more composed than when she went in. Wade watched her paint a smile on her face and curl her hands into fists before she took a few steps toward the dining room. The kiss seemed to have thrown her for a loop. He was glad. Perhaps keeping her off balance was the best thing to do. Kill her with kindness. Use any information Brody came up with to charm her. Being nice might confuse her, make her like him and his family. Maybe then she could understand how important buying the land back was to him.

"Wade, I've put you here," Julianne said, indicating a chair on the far side of the table.

He nodded and made his way over. His sister smiled wickedly at him as she seated Tori next to him and Brody to her left, his good side facing the guest. The rest of the family took their places.

The table was laid with a red-and-gold tablecloth that was barely visible beneath the edge-to-edge casserole dishes, platters and bowls. In the center were thick red pillar candles, poinsettias and golden ribbons that sparkled in the light. As always, Molly had outdone herself.

As tradition dictated, they stood at the table and held hands. Wade reached out and took Tori's hand, trying hard to focus on his father's words instead of how her touch affected him.

"I'm thankful that all of us are back together again. It's been a tough year for everyone," Ken began. "But certainly not the worst we've ever had. We're fighters. We have each been blessed with perseverance and drive and have been brought together for a reason. May we each have a glorious and prosperous New Year and may we each find ourselves back here again next year, blessed in life, love and happiness."

Wade felt Tori gently squeeze his hand. A lump formed in his throat. She understood. At least, she understood his family. She could never truly understand what he was dealing with. He doubted she had such dark secrets buried in her past. Few people did.

Ken smiled. "Merry Christmas, everyone. Let's eat."

Five

Tori was glad she hadn't chickened out after that kiss. She had stood in the bathroom for longer than necessary and toyed with the idea of trying to climb out the tiny window. Reason and hunger trumped her flight reflex, and for that she was grateful. She was stuffed almost as full as the turkey had been before the feasting started. She'd had no idea what a real Christmas dinner was like—one cooked without chafing fuel or charcoal briquettes—until now. There had been mashed potatoes and chestnut-oyster bread stuffing covered in gravy. Maple-glazed carrots. Hot yeast rolls. Then dessert. Good Lord. She'd never known pumpkin pie could melt on your tongue like that.

Everyone had been very friendly, engaging her in their conversations, including Wade. There was a lot of family banter, laughter and tall tales. Tori supposed this was what it was like to have a large family. Growing up as an only child, she'd always longed for a home with a family like this. She'd imagined holidays with merriment and shared stories from childhood.

Tori had sometimes thought that when she married and built her home she'd want to have a lot of children. Four. Maybe five, like the Edens. When things fell apart with Ryan after two years, she'd decided to go ahead and build her dream house anyway. Hopefully love and children would follow. But at the rate she was going, the dreams of that large family were dwindling away. She might end up living in that big house alone.

Perhaps that was why every attempt to start drawing up an architectural design had failed. Even her pen knew there was no point in a home without lively discussion or shared memories to be made there.

Tori turned to listen to Heath as he very animatedly talked about one of his obnoxious advertising clients. They were all such great storytellers. After hearing Ken talk, she knew where the children had learned their skills.

It was a welcome distraction from the night's wildly swirling undercurrents. Having Wade only a few inches away all night had been its own form of torture. She couldn't help but be hyperaware of him. For one thing, he was like a radiator. She could feel the heat of his body penetrating her sweater. Tori tended to run cold, and it took everything she had not to curl against his side and lean into his warmth.

They also kept touching one another. First, holding hands during the blessing before dinner. Then passing food around the table. Without fail their fingers would brush or their shoulders would bump. Innocent, meaningless touches that sent a jolt through her body each time. And the kiss certainly hadn't helped. Whenever

her mind drifted away from dinner, it would go back
to the moment under the mistletoe.

She hadn't expected anything like that. Wade had
had a look on his face as though he were being marched
to the guillotine. Clenched jaw, blank eyes. He hadn't
wanted to kiss her. And yet, once he did…everything
changed. And it really did feel as if everything was
different. In less than a minute the way she thought
about Wade, the way she looked at him, the way she
perceived him shifted on its axis.

Tori dragged her fork through the streaks of whipped
cream left on her dessert plate and pondered the kiss.
There was a tenderness in his touch that surprised
her. A need thrummed through the glide of his fingertips across her skin. It made her want to wrap her
arms around his neck and pull him close. Wade! Of
all the people to make her react like that… A part of
her wished she had found herself under the mistletoe
with any of the other brothers. They were all handsome
and successful. She could do worse, even considering
scowling Brody.

But it had to be Wade, the one she was determined
to keep her defenses up against. He was out to push
her aside and get what he wanted at any price. She had
to remember that.

But somehow that kiss had put a dent in her armor.
Sitting so close to him during dinner, Tori couldn't help
but wonder if he knew it. He'd made it clear that first
night that he would do whatever it took to change her
mind, including seducing her. But the mistletoe kiss
wasn't planned. And she got the feeling from his reaction that it wasn't just a scheme.

So what was that kiss all about? He'd blown off her
question when she asked. She didn't know why. It was

more than just a kiss. More than his ruthless drive. At least, it felt that way to her. Maybe it was just her old attraction to him coloring her impressions.

Tori glanced at Wade beside her. He was watching her. He was facing Heath as his brother talked, but his gaze had strayed to her. There was no anger or animosity in his green eyes. Only desire swirling with the flicker of candlelight. His eyes invited her closer. Dared her to stand under the mistletoe with him again.

No, she had been right. It had been more than just a simple kiss.

Taking a deep breath, Tori turned away and found herself facing Brody. He stiffened when he noticed her move toward him. She could tell he was extremely uncomfortable with her there. While almost everyone else at the table was relaxed and chatting, Brody was board straight in his seat and quiet. He wouldn't look at her, but every now and again his gaze would stray to her, then nervously back to the others at the table.

She hoped she wasn't the cause of his discomfort. Tori would hate it if his holiday was ruined because of her surprise arrival. Why had they seated him beside her if he would be miserable? She didn't know what she could do to make it better. Speaking to him made it worse. So she shifted back toward Wade and felt Brody subtly relax into his chair.

"Can we open a present tonight?" Julianne asked as she got up from the table with a stack of dessert plates she had collected.

"You know the rules," Molly chided. "Only Tori gets her present tonight."

Tori was in the process of standing with her own dish when she paused, hearing her name. "What?"

"Why does Tori get to open her gift?" Heath asked.

"Not once in eighteen years have you ever let one of us open a gift early."

"Stop whining, Heath," Ken said. "Tori is getting her present tonight because she won't be here in the morning when we do gifts."

Tori frowned and pushed in her chair. "No more, please. Having me over for dinner was kind enough, really."

Molly shook her head. "It's too late. If you don't take it, it will be a waste." She turned on her heel and headed into the kitchen, ending the argument.

The next few minutes were a blur of activity. Tori was shooed from the kitchen but watched the activity with interest for a while. Everyone took on a task. Not just the women as she had expected. Wade and Brody pushed up their sleeves and started washing and drying pans. Ken brought in dishes from the dining room. Julianne loaded the dishwasher. Xander loaded plastic containers with extra food. Heath bagged the trash and carried it outside. Molly watched over the process like a tiny drill sergeant.

Feeling useless, Tori went to sit in front of the fireplace. Brody and Heath's fire was quite excellent, and it warmed her back. The old house was beautiful, but a touch drafty, and being near the blaze was a prime spot.

Looking around, she found the same decorating enthusiasm from the gift shop carried over into the house. The fireplace and railing up the stairs were draped in garland. There were candles and poinsettias and other sparkly things everywhere. The tree was the grand centerpiece of the living room. She had expected a tree decorated with coordinating ribbons and glass globes, but this was a family tree. There was a mishmash of ornaments and pieces made with felt, clothespins and glitter glue. Crafts from the children's younger days. Multicolored lights. A shiny gold star on the top. It was perfect.

The rest of the room was equally interesting. There were built-in bookcases filled with leather-bound books, knickknacks and a million picture frames. It was a fascinating thing to Tori. Her family was minimalist out of necessity. They had a strict policy that if they didn't use something for six months, it was gone. And if it didn't serve more than one function, there was no sense in getting it at all.

Tori was distracted by footsteps on the dark hardwood floor. What should've taken at least an hour in the kitchen was done in less than ten minutes. The family poured back into the living room far earlier than Tori had expected.

They all held mugs of cider. Wade had two, one of which he handed to her as he sat down on the stone hearth beside her. She took it with a touch of hesitation. "Did you put something in this?" she asked quietly enough for only him to hear.

He smiled widely, his dangerous charm making it obvious that he could have if he wanted to. "No. Just cider."

With no real choice but to believe him, she sipped the drink. It was warm with cinnamon and caramel undertones. It tasted just the way Christmas should. Not the slightest hint of any chemicals.

"Ken," Molly urged, "go get Tori's gift from the shop, would you, please?"

"I'll get it, Dad." Wade leaped up and beat his father out the door.

Tori sat anxiously awaiting what he was bringing her. He returned a few minutes later with a tiny potted Christmas tree. It was about two feet tall, and it was decorated with tiny balls of birdseed that looked like ornaments, and strands of cranberries and popcorn threaded around it like garland. It was adorably festive and just the right size for her Airstream.

"Is that really for me?" she asked, wishing she had brought something else with the poinsettia. It didn't seem like enough for all their kindness.

"Absolutely," Molly said, beaming with the excitement of gift-giving. "Anyone else would've gotten a larger tree."

Wade approached her with the tree in his arms. "When Mama mentioned you'd never had a Christmas tree, the entire family was rightfully appalled. Everyone needs a Christmas tree, as far as the Edens are concerned." Wade set the tree on the small end table beside her. "This balsam fir is alive and well-potted, so when it's warmer you can plant it somewhere. The decorations are for the birds, quite literally. You can set the tree outside after Christmas, and they'll happily eat up all the decorations so you don't have to find a place to store them."

Tori couldn't help the look of surprise on her face. The gift itself was thoughtful enough, but there was also an attention to detail that she appreciated. These people knew nothing about her, and yet they'd chosen the most perfect present. She didn't know what to say, so she just reached out to touch the ornaments and admire her tree instead of the man who brought it to her.

"It's beautiful," she finally got out. "Thank you for the tree. And for having me to dinner. You may have single-handedly salvaged my holiday."

Wade smiled, and Tori's breath caught in her throat. He'd never smiled at her that way. There was always a challenge, a hard edge of negotiation in his expression, even when he was trying to charm her. Tonight, for the holiday, he seemed to have put that aside. Now his smile was just pure joy. It lit up his face, making him more breathtakingly handsome than he'd ever been.

She swallowed hard and took a sip of her cider to distract herself. Wade sat down beside her again and took up his own mug. Tori held her breath, just knowing that the rapid pound of her heartbeat was loud enough for him to hear sitting so close.

Fortunately, someone suggested Julianne play some carols on the ancient-looking upright piano in the corner. That would be loud enough to muffle the sound. Heath goaded his sister until she took her place at the bench and started playing. She began with "The First Noel," and everyone sat quietly listening to her play.

Tori was relieved to have some time without having to maintain a conversation with someone. She wasn't an introvert, per se, but she did spend a lot of time alone. She'd gotten a little rusty at basic small talk. Eating dinner had taken up a lot of that time until now. Lifting her mug, she happily sipped her mulled cider and listened to the music.

"You may want to leave before too long," Wade suggested.

Tori turned to him with a frown curling her mouth down. Just when she thought they'd called a truce. "Are you ready to be rid of me already?"

"No," he said, turning to the piano and leaning toward her. "But you should know we're hard-core on tradition around here. Once Julianne plays a couple songs, a group of grown men is going to watch *How the Grinch Stole Christmas* on an old VHS tape. Then

Dad will read 'A Visit from Saint Nicholas' to all of us before bed."

Tori smiled. She could hardly imagine a room of powerful CEOs watching cartoons. "It sounds sweet. Are there footie pajamas involved?"

"No, thankfully they don't make them in my size. When we were kids, yeah, it was cute. Now it's just getting old and sad, but we haven't provided the requisite grandchildren to pass on the tradition."

"Mmm..." she murmured, taking the last sip of her cider as the final notes of Julianne's song rang out. "I'd better go, then."

"I'll walk you out. My mom is loading you down with leftovers, so I'll carry your tree."

Tori arched an eyebrow at Wade but didn't argue. As she rose, Molly got up as well, and the two women headed into the kitchen where Tori disposed of her mug in the sink. Wade was right: Molly had packed a bag full of containers to feed her for a few days. Molly gave Tori a big hug, thanked her for coming and walked her to the door.

Tori was careful to avoid the mistletoe this time as she grabbed her coat and flung it over her arm. She waved good-night to everyone, then headed out the door with Wade behind her.

They crunched through the snow to where she'd parked her truck without saying a word. She unlocked the passenger door and set the leftovers on the floorboard. Wade put the tree on the bench, and Tori fastened it into place with the seat belt. "That should hold it steady," she said, tossing her bulky jacket inside and slamming the heavy door closed.

Wade was standing beside her, leaning casually against the truck. She expected him to go back into the house—he didn't even have his coat on—but he stayed firmly in place. His green eyes were black in the dark night, fixed on her face. The intensity of his gaze made her skin flush and a tingle run down the length of her spine.

"That wasn't so bad, was it?" she teased, unsure what else to say with him watching her so closely.

"No, it wasn't. I rather enjoyed it. I hope you had a good time. My family seems to like you."

"I did have a good time. They seem like really great people."

"They are. I would do anything to protect them."

Tori felt the mood shift. He wasn't just talking about Christmas dinner anymore. She'd hoped they could shelve this argument for at least one night.

"I know there's a part of you that thinks I'm the big bad wolf out to steal your property. The fact of the matter is that without getting lawyers involved and doing some fairly ugly things that would hurt my parents and their reputation, I can't take this land from you. And I can't force you to sell it. But I hope that meeting my family tonight helps you understand where I'm coming from and how important this is to me. So you know that I've been telling you the truth the whole time."

Wade took a step forward, invading her space. If he was deliberately trying to use his size to intimidate her, his plan was backfiring. She was anything but intimidated. When he was that close, she was thoroughly turned on and extremely distracted from the conversation.

"I need you…" he began, wrapping a gentle hand around her upper arm. Tori couldn't help leaning in to him, her brain short-circuiting with his touch and his words. "…to believe me, Tori."

Tori sighed, an expression of disappointment wrinkling her delicate nose. "Wade, what difference does it make if I believe you or not? You want my land. I don't want to sell it to you. It's a fairly cut-and-dried scenario."

Wade shrugged. "Nothing is that simple. Years of experience have taught me that there is always room to negotiate. Everyone has a pressure point. For some people, it's a dollar amount. That's obviously not the case with you or we would've resolved this the first day. I didn't plan for you to be here tonight, but maybe some good can come of it. Perhaps you have a soft spot for family that would help you understand. I don't want to be the bad guy. I like you, Tori. You're spunky. And beautiful when you aren't pointing a gun at me."

He watched Tori's eyes widen and her mouth softly part at his compliment. "You're just flattering me to get your way," she accused, shrugging off his hand.

"I won't lie to you. I do want the land. But I also want to get to know you better. And for you to like me. I'd like to ask you out to dinner sometime. A nice romantic dinner without my family's prying eyes watching our every move. The perfect scenario ends with both of us achieving everything we want."

"How do you know anything about what I want?"

Wade looked into Tori's eyes. They reflected a confusion he could sense in every inch of her tense body language. She wanted him. She despised him. He was walking a fine line between the two sides. He decided to push her until her desire won the battle. He leaned in and gently brushed a strand of red hair out of her face, barely grazing her forehead and cheek with his fingertips. Tori sucked in a ragged breath when he touched her. He spoke low, almost like a lover's whisper. "Maybe I don't. So tell me, what do you want, Tori?"

She swallowed hard but didn't pull away from him. "I want…" Her voice trailed away as though she couldn't find the right words. "I didn't think you'd stoop so low as to try to romance the land out from under me," she replied, choosing to ignore his question. "As if you even could."

So she was onto him. That might make the seduction harder, but not impossible. "You doubt my abilities?" He grinned a wide, mischievous smile at her and pulled back to give her some room to breathe. He'd rattled her enough.

"No, but perhaps you underestimate my ability to resist you. Tell me, what was that kiss about?"

That was a damn good question. What *was* that kiss about? Tori was the last woman he needed to be attracted to, but his reaction to her was undeniable. Stupid, but undeniable. At best, he could try to use their attraction to tip the scales in his favor. "I told you already. I'm after the win-win scenario."

"I'm not going to sell you my land, Wade. If that's all tonight was about, all that kiss was about, then you can take your Christmas tree and go back inside."

Tori shifted her boots in the snow and crossed her arms under her breasts. The act of defiance did little to discourage the thoughts about her running through his mind. It had only focused his brain on the perky orbs of her breasts that pressed against her chenille sweater and threatened to erupt over the top of her scoop neckline.

It made his mouth water to think about gliding his hands over the soft fabric and kneading her supple flesh. He had the fierce urge to run his tongue along her collarbone and the crest of her breasts.

When he tore his gaze away and looked her in the eye again, he knew he'd been caught in the act. Her eyes widened, and he was struck by what a gorgeous shade of blue they were. Her eyes were a lovely shade of light blue that reminded him of the ice-blue eyes of his friend's Siberian husky. Cool, wary and penetrating. They were also sparkling with the hint of a desire she didn't want to acknowledge. She dropped her hands back to her sides to ruin the display she created.

"Actually, no. That isn't all that it's about." He didn't elaborate, but the pointed way he watched her lips as she tentatively licked them should have spelled it out for her.

Whether it was due to the cold or to his blatant admiration, her creamy cheeks turned a rosy pink and her breath came out rapidly in foglike bursts. He wondered if that was how she would look when she was flushed and breathless from his passionate caresses.

He hadn't been lying when he said he wanted her to like him. That he wanted to ask her out to dinner sometime. When they argued, his blood boiled with irritation and arousal all at once. Wade liked a challenge. Tori was certainly that.

Sure, he intended to get that land back one way or another, but that was a separate issue. Business versus pleasure. He wished she could see the difference, but the women he'd known had a tendency to tangle issues together into an impossible knot. Tori was no different where this was concerned.

Initially he'd thought that indulging in their undeniable connection would complicate the issue. But kissing her in the foyer had changed everything. Denying the electricity between them might actually make their problems worse. He was certainly getting cranky returning to his bunkhouse room every night, alone, with Tori on his mind. Tonight he would have to share the room with Brody and listen to his opinion on the matter.

That wouldn't help the tension building up, either. Perhaps if he and Tori blew off a little steam together, the situation wouldn't seem quite so dire. On her end, at least. On his end, it was most certainly dire, no matter how much pent-up sexual frustration taunted him.

His perfect solution would be to get the land back, offer her enough money that she could buy land that was even better for her needs, and have her in his bed for a while. There didn't have to be a bad guy in this story if she would be open-minded to the options. He wasn't above abusing their sexual chemistry to get his way—if they happened to end up in bed together, so be it.

And at the moment, he wished it would happen sooner rather than later.

"This is also about the chemistry between us." Wade took another step toward her and she didn't back away. His hand went to her face, tipping her chin up to look at him. Even in heeled boots, she had to strain to look him in the eye this close. "I'm not the only one to feel it, am I?"

Tori gave just a subtle shake of her head. He could detect it only by his hand against her smooth skin. "I feel it," she whispered.

She stepped closer until their bodies were nearly touching. He was suddenly aware of the scent of her perfume again, an alluring earthy and floral mix. It made his whole body tighten with anticipation of touching her the way he'd wanted to earlier but couldn't. Now he was free to act without the eyes of his family and their obnoxious critiques.

Wade didn't need any more of an invitation. He dived into her, capturing her lips and cupping her up-turned face in his hands. She was soft and open to him.

He felt her hands press against his chest, not to push him away, but to feel him through the thick wool of his sweater. Wade moaned against her mouth as her silky tongue glided along his own. It sent a sharp barb of pleasure through his body, urging him to take more than he should tonight. His hands fell from her face to slip around her waist. He tugged her to him, relishing the feel of her soft body against his hard angles.

Without pulling away, he inched them backward through the snow until her back was pressed against the cold metal of her truck door. She gasped but didn't resist it. In fact, it seemed to light a fire in her. When his mouth left hers to finally taste the hollow of her throat, Tori wrapped her arms around his neck, her silky stocking-clad leg sliding up the outside of his thigh to hook around his hip and draw him in.

The throbbing of his groin pressing into her was almost as uncomfortable as the needling cold on his exposed skin. His hot lips scorched across her frosty throat in a delicious contrast. It wasn't until her pebble-hard nipples pressed into his chest that reality intruded. He was practically devouring her in twenty-degree weather, and neither of them had on a coat.

Forcing himself to pull away, he took one last gentle kiss and backed off. Wade sucked in a large breath of painfully icy air to kill his arousal. He couldn't walk back into the house like this. He grabbed her upper arms and pulled her away from the frigid metal siding of her truck. "I'm sorry," he said. "You've got to be freezing. I didn't think about that at the time."

"To the contrary," she said, her lips swollen and her

cheeks still red. "I'm feeling quite warm for some reason." She smiled sheepishly and brushed a long strand of red hair behind her ear.

Damn. He'd forgotten to touch her hair. He'd ached to do that from the first moment he saw it.

"You don't have a coat on, either," she said. "You'd better get back inside or you'll spend your Christmas Day sick instead of with your family. You don't want to miss the Grinch."

Wade smiled and shook his head. "I'm certain they'll wait for me, whether I want them to or not." There were unnecessary words swirling in his gut that he had the urge to say before he left. They probably wouldn't help the situation, but he couldn't keep them inside. "I want you to know that all this doesn't have anything to do with the land."

Tori stood on her toes to press a soft goodbye kiss to his lips. "I know," she whispered faintly against his mouth.

He had to force his hands into fists buried deep in his pant pockets to keep from reaching for her again.

"I'm glad this one wasn't in front of your whole family," she said with a grin. Before he could respond, Tori turned and ran around to the other side of the truck. "Merry Christmas, Wade." She climbed inside and the engine roared to life.

Tori gave a quick wave as she turned her truck and pulled away from the Garden of Eden. Wade watched her disappear into the darkness, and then ran his hand through his hair.

"Merry Christmas, Tori."

Six

Thursday night, Tori sat in her favorite seat at the counter of Daisy's Diner. Now that the holiday had passed and the leftovers Molly forced on her were all eaten, it was back to her usual haunt.

Over the past few weeks she'd made her first friend in the waitress who handled the counter there. Her name tag said "Rosalyn," but she told Tori to just call her Rose. Rose was off on Wednesday nights, but any other day of the week Tori would be at Daisy's for dinner.

"Hey there, Tori. What will it be tonight?" Rose asked, leaning casually against the countertop.

Her eyes barely glanced at the menu before she made her decision. "How about the chicken pot pie and some hot tea?"

Rose smiled. "You got it." She spun from the counter and disappeared into the back, returning a few minutes later with a teacup and a small kettle of hot water. "I'm surprised you didn't starve over the holiday with us closed," Rose said with a smile.

"I was able to depend on the kindness of strangers," Tori admitted. "The Edens invited me over for dinner."

Rose perked up in quite a peculiar way. "The Edens, huh? Are they *all* in town for Christmas?"

"Yes. At least they were. I met all of them on Christmas Eve. Some of them may have left by now."

The waitress nodded, a hint of disappointment in her dark brown eyes. She turned and Tori followed Rose's line of sight to where her son was sitting alone in a corner booth. The little boy was eight or nine, and whenever Tori came in, he was doing homework or playing his handheld video games while Rose worked.

"I always had a soft spot for Xander. We dated on and off in high school before he left for college. He had a smile that would make my heart just melt. Very charming. It's no wonder he's a politician. He has a way with people."

Tori nodded in agreement. "He was very nice. I was more worried about Wade, though. He's been giving me some trouble."

"Worried? Why? My sister went to high school with him." A sly grin spread across Rose's face. "A lot of women in this town wouldn't mind Wade Mitchell giving them trouble. Some say he's the pick of the litter."

Tori chuckled, a hint of bitterness beneath it. "Well, those people would say differently if they had something he wanted. He's very persistent and downright irritating when he doesn't get his way."

"What could you possibly have that he wants? You just got here."

"He wants my land."

Rose frowned. "The land you just bought?"

She nodded and sipped her tea. "It belonged to his family and he wants to buy it back."

"I don't know why he'd want it. None of the kids have ever shown much interest in the farm. But I'll tell you, if I had to have someone causing me trouble, I'd take an Eden boy in a heartbeat. At least you'd have something nice to look at while you suffered."

That was certainly true. All the Eden boys were attractive. Even Brody, if you could look past the scars and the attitude. If given her choice of the lot, the decision wouldn't be difficult. Wade was certainly her type: dark hair, soulful eyes, a wicked smile... Unfortunately, the magnificent view was a distraction she couldn't afford. "As nice as that all sounds, he's becoming a major pain in my—"

"Well, speak of the devil." Rose straightened immediately and started fidgeting with her dark brown ponytail. Tori turned in her seat and found Wade there, hanging up his coat on a rack by the door. She turned back before he could see her, hoping he wouldn't notice her. Unfortunately, Rose was strutting around so conspicuously in front of her that he was certain to look her way eventually.

"Hey, Rosie," Wade said, sitting down at the counter a few seats away. "How've you been?"

Rose slid down the counter as if she'd been pulled in by his tractor beam. "Good. How about you?"

"Busy. How's your dad doing these days?"

Tori watched the smile fade from Rose's face. "He's okay. I'm sure he's bored out of his skull, but twenty-three hours a day in a cell will do that to you."

Wade straightened in surprise. Apparently he hadn't kept up with the latest Cornwall gossip. Even Tori knew that Rose's dad had gone to jail last year. She didn't know what for, exactly, but it didn't sound as though he would be getting out anytime soon.

"Oh, I hadn't heard he was, uh… I'm sorry. *Um*…do you guys have the pot roast special tonight?"

Rose smiled again and let the uncomfortable subject drop. "That's only on Mondays. But we've got the sliced roast beef with mushroom gravy and mashed potatoes. It's almost as good."

"That'll do. And a lemon-lime soda, please."

"You bet." Rose shot Tori a wink and disappeared into the kitchen.

Alone at the counter with him, Tori couldn't decide if she should shrink into herself and hope she became invisible or sit up tall and dare him to say something to her. She hadn't seen him since Christmas Eve. Since they kissed. And now she didn't quite know how to act. Was he still the enemy? Her body didn't think so, but her brain disagreed. He could be exploiting their natural attraction to get his way. She would have to err on the side of caution and continue under the assumption he was the enemy, kisses or no, until he stopped asking to buy her land. She couldn't trust his motives.

And yet she didn't want to fight with him anymore. It was all too confusing.

She opted for a happy medium, quietly sipping her tea and waiting for her dinner to arrive. Tori focused so intently on it that she noticed only a familiar heat, and when she looked up, Wade was on the stool beside her. She hadn't even realized he'd moved.

"Hello, Tori."

She turned in her seat to look at him. He was wearing dark tailored jeans and a black cashmere sweater that fit his broad shoulders beautifully. She itched to reach out and brush the soft fabric as an excuse to touch him again.

"Wade," she responded simply. She was afraid she'd give away too much if she said anything more.

Wade smiled broadly, undeterred by her cool reception. He took the drink Rose offered him before she disappeared into the kitchen again, leaving Tori high and dry. He took a sip before he spoke. "Do you eat here a lot?"

"Most nights. You've seen my kitchen." She was certain her confusion was etched on her face, but there was nothing she could do about it. "You're awfully friendly tonight."

"Why wouldn't I be? The last time I saw you, we made out against the side of your truck."

Tori's cheeks lit up as bright as her hair. "Don't say it like that," she said, wishing her pot pie would come and give her something to focus on instead of her memories of making out with Wade. She couldn't think of anything else with his scent so close, tempting her to do it again.

Wade grinned and she was glad she was sitting down and didn't have to worry about her knees giving out from under her. She wished she didn't amuse him so much. If he smiled less and sat farther away, she might not be fighting this pointless attraction to the man she was trying very hard not to like. A man she *shouldn't* like, considering he fired her, made her lose her apartment and was hell-bent on taking away her second chance at settling down.

It was that stupid smile that did it.

"Okay," he agreed, leaning in to whisper the words softly in her ear. "The last time I saw you, I drank in your lips like a sweet wine I couldn't get enough of."

Rose approached at that moment, heard Wade's low words, then immediately spun on her heel and vanished. Tori knew she'd hear more about that later, but she could hardly care with Wade's deep voice vibrating through her. A shiver ran down Tori's spine when he spoke, and gooseflesh drew up all over her skin. His warm breath on her neck took her back to the snow, to the truck, to the kisses she couldn't forget. Why did he have this power over her? "I s-suppose that's a better way to put it," she stuttered. "And yet you haven't darkened my doorstep since then."

"I wanted to, believe me. But I had to put in the family time. We only get together once a year. The last of them left today, so I'm free to begin harassing you again."

Honestly, she'd felt his presence even with him gone. The past few days he'd plagued her thoughts, overrun her dreams and disrupted her focus. Memories of his kisses lingered. She was on edge thinking he might show up any minute to continue his petition to buy the land. Or better yet, to pick up where they'd left off. He might as well have been sitting in her camper since Monday night.

"Why did you stay behind when the others left?" she said, pushing the thoughts of his touch out of her mind.

"A few things needed my attention," he said.

She swallowed hard. "Like what?"

"Like you." His lips curled in a smug grin. He knew he was pushing all the right buttons. "So how long have you been here in Cornwall?"

The change in discussion nearly gave her whiplash, but the topic was thankfully a safe one. "Two months. I had been looking at this area for a while before that but hadn't found any land that suited the house I want to build."

"Shouldn't an architect build a house to suit the land, not the other way around?"

"Perhaps." She shrugged. "But this is going to be my one and only home. The place where I live for the rest of my life. I've been thinking about what I want for years, and I finally have the money and time to make it happen. That plot of land is perfect for what I envision. I refuse to settle."

"Understandable. How are the plans coming for the house?"

Tori's lips twisted with concern before she spoke. "Not as quickly as I'd like. But you can't rush perfection. I hope to have the blueprints finalized this week and break ground before the end of January."

Wade's eyes widened almost imperceptibly and his brow furrowed with thoughts he didn't choose to share. "Why Cornwall? You're not from around here, are you?"

"No and yes. I'm not from anywhere. My parents and I traveled my whole life. But I came to visit this area on a long weekend while I was working in Philadelphia, and I fell in love with it."

Wade was listening intently, and it bothered her. The conversation seemed innocent enough. What was his angle? He couldn't really care. Was he just making small talk or was he trying to get information he could use against her later? Maybe he'd try to stall her building permits and frustrate her into selling.

"I've lived around here my whole life."

"Cornwall?"

"Not exactly. Here and there in Litchfield County. I bounced around through a lot of different foster homes at first. I came to Cornwall when I was ten and stayed here until I went off to Yale."

"Is that where you met Stanton?" Alex Stanton had been Wade's business partner when she first went to work for him.

"Yes. We started our own company together after college, and then after you left, we decided to split up and focus on different types of projects. He wanted to branch out, go nationwide and, eventually, international. I wanted to focus on Manhattan, so I've been on my own a few years now."

"Now the two of you can make money twice as fast."

"Precisely the idea behind our dastardly plan."

Damned if she didn't smile at him. He had a way of making her like him no matter how badly she didn't want to. He was only a few days into his petition and he had already managed to charm her. He'd kissed her. How long could she hold out against this? How long until he tired and gave up?

"So, tell me about some of your green innovations. I've been hoping to add more into my projects."

At that, Tori outright frowned. He really was taking every available angle to butter her up. "Really?"

"Yes, really. I've been investing heavily in a couple of green companies over the past few years. They're really making some great strides in products that are earth friendly and, I hope soon, affordable for consumers. I think more people will use them when the price isn't so intimidating."

That surprised her. When you're in the business of renovating and reselling buildings, every penny spent cuts into the profit. She never expected him to be the kind who would invest in green products. But she was glad he did. She wished more people would. "I agree.

That's why I try to get as much exposure for my work as possible. I want to increase interest and demand, which will hopefully make some of these innovations mainstream and drive down the price."

"It's hard to do. My folks have managed to run an organic farm without the crippling prices breaking their profit margin, but it's taken decades to perfect it."

Tori's brows shot up over her teacup. "The tree farm is organic?"

"For the past twenty years."

Wade was full of good surprises tonight. She wouldn't admit it to anyone, but she was actually enjoying her conversation with him. It felt almost like a fun, casual first date.

Did she just use the word date?

"I've been looking at some of your recent projects online. You really do great work. The building in Philadelphia is stunning."

Tori blushed again. If he was playing her, he was good at it. She couldn't help but believe him. Her latest project really was incredible. Her best apart from her own house, which was going to be her greatest work. "Thank you. It's almost done. The ribbon cutting is scheduled for just after the New Year."

"I wish we hadn't lost you at our company. Your talents would've been put to good use."

It sounded like a compliment, but this time it rubbed her the wrong way. Tori was about to say something rude about how he shouldn't have fired her, but Rose returned then, placing a piping-hot dish of chicken pot pie on the counter in front of her. It was the perfect opportunity for her to focus on something else.

The pie had a golden flaky crust that Tori yearned to bust open with her fork. Typically, she'd leaned toward club sandwiches and grilled chicken plates, but dinner with the Edens had been a gateway meal. Now she was on a personal mission to make up for twenty-eight years of home-cooking deprivation.

"That smells great," he said, leaning closer to her and inhaling the enticing aroma. "Don't let me stop you from enjoying your meal."

Tori opened her mouth to argue with him about etiquette, but Rose came by with his plate, too. Now she couldn't even refuse out of politeness.

"Perfect," he said, eyeing his roast beef. "Now we can eat together. Not exactly what I envisioned for our first date, but it will do."

"Date?" Tori's head snapped up from her plate. The man must be reading her mind. It was the only answer.

"I told you I wanted to take you out to dinner," he said before popping a bite of beef into his mouth and swallowing. "I was thinking more of wine and candlelight, but we can save that for our second date."

"We're dating now?" It was news to her. News that made her heart flutter momentarily in her chest as though she were a teenager.

Wade shrugged. "Why label it? We're just enjoying each other's company and getting to know one another. What are you doing tomorrow night?"

Tori paused with a bite of chicken and vegetables in midair. "Why?"

Dropping his fork to his plate, Wade spun on his stool to face her. His brow was furrowed with irritation, but the light in his green eyes indicated it was more exasperation than anything else. "Why must you make everything so difficult? It's a simple question. Do you have plans Friday night or not?"

"No." It was the truth. She worked during the day

on the blueprints for the house, fielding calls and holding virtual meetings on other projects, but most of her evenings were spent reading or messing around on her computer until she got sleepy.

"Well, you do now. I'm going to take you out on a proper dinner date."

Wade had to admit this was the first time he'd ever dressed in an Armani suit, gotten into his BMW and driven to a trailer to pick up a woman for dinner. As he climbed out of the SUV, he was pleased that the sunny day, while cold, had managed to melt most of the snow and reveal the well-packed gravel of her temporary driveway. A couple more warm days and he might be able to find the turtle-shaped rock on her property that served as a makeshift headstone.

He had tried to talk himself into canceling this date several times today. He was attracted to Tori, but he could suppress that urge if he needed to. Asking her out had very little to do with his desire for her. As much as he didn't like the idea, getting close to Tori was the best way to soften her up. She'd gone from a hellcat to a kitten after spending time with his family. The information Brody had supplied him with about her business had made her putty in his hands. He was confident that a date or two would wear her down.

It had to. If Tori intended to break ground on the house in a few weeks' time, he had to hurry. There wasn't time to finesse this situation. He had to win Tori over one way or another, and this seemed to be the quickest way. She was attracted to him. If the past was any indication, that might be enough to influence her decision.

It was sleazy. Underhanded. And absolutely necessary. He couldn't fail his family.

As he made his way to her front door, he enjoyed feeling the crunch of gravel against the soles of his dress shoes. He'd opted not to wear his snow boots and was hoping Tori had done the same. The knee-high boots she'd worn at Christmas were nice, but he was a self-proclaimed ankle guy. Just another reason for him to despise the cold and ice of New England winters. His favorite part of the female body was tucked away until spring.

He had his fingers crossed that she would step out of that Airstream in one of her sexy pairs of heels. Back when she'd worked for him, he could always count on finding her near the copier or in the break room wearing an attractive yet professional outfit and a pair of luscious heels. It had been the highlight of his day.

He gave a quick rap on the aluminum door and waited for her to answer. A moment later it swung open, and he stepped back to hold it for her. Cling to it was more like it.

The elevated camper gave him a prime view of a pair of black patent leather pumps with a strap around each delicate ankle. His heart almost skipped a beat as his gaze traveled up the length of her calves to the dark red bandage dress that clung to her round, full hips. The neckline was off the shoulder, and dipped low to give a tantalizing yet tasteful view of her breasts.

Tori smiled and slipped into a black full-length wool coat before stepping down to join him. Her thick auburn hair was swept up into a twist, exposing the long, pale line of her neck and sparkling ruby earrings. Her pale eyes looked mysterious and exotic lined in black with a smoky shadow.

She was, in a word, breathtaking.

He reached out a hand to help her down the stairs and then pushed the door shut behind her. "You look beautiful," he said.

"Thank you," Tori replied. The blush of her cheeks was made even more evident by the powerful red of her dress peeking out from under her coat. "You look very nice, too. I don't think I've seen you in a suit since we worked together."

Wade smiled and held out his arm to lead her to the passenger side of his car. "I wear them all the time in real life. On the farm, I'd just get pine sap on it. More rugged attire is required out here, as you know."

Tori eased into the heated leather seat and pulled her legs in. "Yes, these heels aren't very practical in the country."

"That's a damn shame," Wade said as he slammed her door closed. He then got in on his side.

Tori waited until they were on the highway before she spoke again. "So where are we going?"

"A little French place I know on the west side. It's a far cry from Daisy's Diner, I have to tell you."

"Wait, I think I've heard of that place. Incredible food, but almost impossible to get in?"

"That's the place."

"How did you get reservations? You just asked me out last night. It's Friday, one of the busiest nights. I've heard people can wait months for a table."

Wade turned to her with his cockiest smile. "I know people."

"Oh, that's very impressive," she mocked.

"I went to high school with the executive chef. We've stayed good friends over the years. Whenever I'm in town, all I have to do is call and I've got a table held for me."

"That must go over well with all the women you take there."

Wade tried not to make a face, but he couldn't help it. She made him sound like a tomcat running around west Connecticut. "I'm usually alone or with one of my brothers," he said. "I think this is the first date I've ever taken there. I'm usually not in Cornwall long enough to romance anyone."

Tori nodded and turned to glance out the window at the rapidly darkening sky. "So when do you head back to the big bad city?"

"I don't know," Wade admitted.

And he didn't know. His plan had been to secure the land, spend Christmas with his family and hop the next plane to Jamaica. He should be gone by now, but that hadn't panned out. All his brothers and Julianne had returned to their respective homes. And he was still there. Without the land. And without a ticket to a warm tropical locale.

When all this was over, he was going to demand a vacation on Brody's private Caribbean island. He owed Wade after all the grief he'd served him the past few days.

"Don't you have a business to get back to?"

"Not until after the New Year. My company shuts down for two weeks so my employees can enjoy the holidays."

"Was it your intention to spend those two weeks here, badgering me?"

"No. By now I'd intended to be on a beach, soaking in the sun and badgering a waitress for another drink."

Tori turned to him. "So you'll stay in Cornwall until you wear me down, right?"

Wade met her gaze momentarily before turning back to the road. "Yes."

"And what if I deliberately stalled just to keep you around?"

Wade slowed the SUV to turn into the parking lot of the restaurant. For a packed night, there weren't many cars, but the dining room was small and didn't have many tables. Or a menu, for that matter. They served a series of tasting courses, chef's choice. Wade pulled into a spot and turned off the car.

Unbuckling his seat belt, he pivoted to face her. "If you're really interested in keeping me around, there are better ways to go about it."

"Like what?" she asked. The challenge lighted her eyes like sparkling hunks of aquamarine.

"Like making wild, passionate love to me until I can't bear to leave your side."

Tori's mouth dropped open. Her lips moved in vain for a moment, but there were no words. He seemed to have that effect on her, and he had to admit he liked it. Wade grinned wickedly and climbed from the car. He came around and opened the door for her, taking her hand as she slid from the seat.

They walked to the restaurant with his arm around her waist. He liked the feel of her body against his side. She fit perfectly there, and he needed only to turn his head toward her to breathe in the floral scent of her shampoo. It made him want to spread the strands across a silky pillowcase and bury his face in them. Soon. Hopefully.

Just as they opened the door, he leaned in and whispered, "And I hope you'll put that new plan into place tonight after dessert."

The sounds of the restaurant eclipsed any response she might have cobbled together. He focused instead on greeting the hostess, the executive chef's wife, and following her to an intimate table for two by the fireplace. Wade helped Tori out of her coat, then handed both their jackets over to the hostess to be checked.

Moments later their server, Richard, arrived with two glasses of white wine. After welcoming them and introducing himself, he placed the glasses on the table, adding, "We're starting tonight with an '83 sauvignon blanc and a tasting of caviar and white asparagus."

A second server swooped in behind Richard with their first plates, and then both of them disappeared into the kitchen.

"I hope you're hungry," Wade said, admiring the artistry of their first dish. "There's nine more courses."

They'd need every bit of spare room to eat all the food and wine presented to them. There was a *fois gras* terrine, butter-poached lobster, potatoes with black truffles, lamb, sorbet and the most delicate white chocolate mousse with cherries he'd ever put into his mouth. The food and wine flowed as easily as their conversation.

Wade had been concerned at first that their usual antagonistic banter might ruin the evening. As much as fighting with Tori aroused him, he wanted tonight to be about something else. The more she got to know him, the more she seemed to open up to him. The information Brody had been able to uncover about Tori had proved fairly useful so far. Talking about her work and her passion for environmental causes had opened a door to him.

Tonight the romantic atmosphere and the multiple courses of wine seemed to help her relax and enjoy herself. After about the third course, he could see the tension ease from her shoulders and a lazy pleasure settle into her eyes. She laughed and flirted, smiled and watched him over her glass with warmth in her gaze. He liked this side of Tori just as much as, if not more than, her fiery red side.

They talked about their work and their college experiences. Tori shared details about her travels as a child and all the things she'd seen. Wade had to admit he was a touch jealous that she had seen so many things at such a young age. When he was young, he was poor. And now that he was no longer poor, he was too busy to travel.

In turn she asked him a lot about his high school years and growing up with brothers and sisters. They had lived quite different lives.

Before he knew it, he looked up and found they were the only customers left in the restaurant. There was only the sultry music playing in the background and the crackling of the fireplace beside them. Even the servers seemed to blend into the background, well-trained not to interfere with their customers' romantic evenings.

"Did you say you never went to prom?"

Tori looked up from her last half-eaten plate. "No prom. No high school graduation. None of the normal stuff."

"Do you like to dance?"

She hesitated a moment before she answered. "I don't know. I've never actually danced with a man before. I mean, I went to a few nightclubs in college, but not real dancing. There's never really been the opportunity. No school dances, no family weddings…"

Wade frowned and eyed the area just beside their table. "That is a travesty." He stood, placing his napkin in his seat, and reached out for Tori's hand. "Come here."

Despite a flash of wariness in her eyes, Tori didn't argue with his demand, and he was glad. Instead, she rose gracefully from her chair and took the few steps over to the open area that was the perfect dance floor for two.

Wade pulled her into his arms, giving her time to adjust to the proper stance before pressing her body against his own and rocking in gentle time with the music. At first she was stiff in his arms. He worried that it was him, but her glance kept nervously shifting down to her feet. She was uncomfortable not knowing how to dance.

"I don't think I'm very good at this," she said, worrying her lip with her teeth.

"Just relax," he cooed into her ear. "No one is watching. It's only you and me." Wade splayed his hand across her lower back, pressing her into him and guiding her movements. "Close your eyes and feel the music. Feel the movement."

Tori closed her eyes, her body relaxing after a few moments. Then she leaned in and placed her head on his shoulder. Wade reveled in the feel of her in his arms, closing his own eyes to block out everything but the experience of holding her.

Her skin was like satin against his. The soft curves of her body fit into each hard ridge of his own. He could feel the crush of her breasts against the wall of his chest and the rapidly beating heart behind it. The rhythm of it matched the pounding in his own rib cage. The blood had started rushing in his veins the moment he touched her. Every nerve in his body was tingling with arousal and anxiety.

Despite all the complications and reasons he shouldn't want Tori, he did. He wanted her very badly. And he was fairly certain she felt the same way.

Tori shifted in his arms, and he opened his eyes to see her pull away just enough to look him in the eye.

"I'm ready," she said.

"For what?"

The corners of her red lips curled up in a seductive smile. "To make you never want to leave my side again."

Seven

Tori had never seen a man pay a check so quickly. A wad of large bills was tossed onto the table, and he grasped her hand to lead her out of the restaurant. They paused only long enough to collect their coats, and then they were back on the road.

Whereas on the way to the restaurant his engine had purred, now the German motor roared and devoured the highway ahead of them. The speed only fueled the desire burning inside her. Its flames licked at her skin, flushing her pink and melting her core into a pool of liquid need. She wasn't exactly sure where they were going, but she didn't care. She just wanted to get there fast.

Her left hand crept across the gap between them and planted itself firmly on his thigh. Her fingers rubbed over the soft material of his suit, his muscles tensing beneath her grip. The speedometer surged in response, and the reaction urged her on. She stroked his leg, inching ever higher.

When she glanced up at Wade, his face was rock hard, his jaw locked and his eyes burrowing into the road. His knuckles were white as they gripped the leather steering wheel. He was fighting hard for control. So far, he seemed to have it managed.

That made Tori want to push him. The road was deserted and dark. With a wicked smile, she moved her hand higher, dipping between his thighs. She found the firm heat of him struggling against the confines of his pants. Wade jerked and groaned at her touch, but the SUV remained steady and in control as they traveled.

With curious fingertips she explored him. She gently stroked his length and swallowed hard when he extended beyond her expectations. She wet her lips in anticipation and clamped her thighs tightly together to quell the ache building inside her. She wanted him so badly. Even back when she was his employee, she'd fantasized about this. At least before…

No. She wasn't going to ruin tonight with thoughts about the past. She'd always wanted a taste of Wade Mitchell, and tonight she was going to have it. When she spied the apple-shaped sign of the tree farm, a rush of relief washed over her. They were almost there.

As the SUV's tires met the gravel of the driveway, Tori palmed his fly with one last firm stroke. Wade growled low, whipping the car to a stop. They'd parked in front of a building that looked like a barn, but without the hayloft, large swinging doors and livestock. Thank goodness they weren't heading to the big house. As much as she wanted him, she just couldn't… Not there with Ken and Molly so close by.

The engine went quiet. Wade stretched his hands to

relax the tense muscles and turned in his seat. His gaze dropped to her hand, which was still touching him, and shifted back up to meet hers. "I've got to get you in the house before I'm forced to make love to you in the backseat like a teenage boy."

Instead of responding, Tori gave him another firm squeeze. Wade's hand grabbed her wrist and tugged her away before she could move again. "No, seriously," he said, his eyes closed. "It's not very comfortable back there."

"Okay," Tori agreed with a grin. "But only because having sex in a bedroom without wheels is a rare treat for me." With a laugh, she climbed out of the SUV, too anxious to wait for him to open her door. He met her around the other side and took her hand, leading her to the front door.

Once inside the building, Wade locked the dead bolt behind them and swept her into his arms. His mouth crushed hers, devouring her with an enthusiasm her body had been craving since their fourth course. Tori let her purse fall to the ground and wrapped her arms around his neck. She was glad she'd chosen to wear these heels, because they brought his mouth closer to hers and aligned their bodies perfectly. His erection pressed into her lower belly, and she tilted her hips to grind against it. A growl vibrated across her lips, followed by the glide of his tongue along hers.

Wade's hands moved up her back until they reached her zipper. A hum ran along her spine to the base as it glided down and exposed her back to the cool air. His fingers delved beneath the fabric to caress her skin and undo the snaps of her strapless bra.

As much as she hated to break away from him, she knew she needed to if she wanted to feel her bare skin on his. Tori pressed against his chest until his lips left hers. His warm hands cupped her shoulders, pushing her dress down until it pooled around her ankles with her bra. Now she was wearing only her lace panties, sheer thigh-high stockings and heels. She could feel his eyes on her, drinking in every inch of her body. Tori thought she would feel self-conscious, but the fire in his eyes was undeniable. He wanted her. There might be other layers of conflict between them, but his desire was genuine.

To tempt him, she reached behind her head to pull out the few pins that held her hair in the twist. Her breasts reached out to him as she moved, the tight nipples aching for his touch. His gaze went to them, his tongue darting across his lower lip as he watched. Instead of reaching for her, he tugged down his tie and threw it to the ground.

Once the pins were removed, the thick red curls fell down over her bare shoulders. She gently shook her head and stepped out of her dress.

"God, you're beautiful," he said, his voice a hoarse whisper. "Come here."

Tori closed the gap between them. Her palms ran over his chest and up to his shoulders to slip his jacket off. It fell to the floor beside his tie, and Tori made quick work of the dress shirt buttons.

When Wade shrugged out of his shirt, Tori's breath caught in her throat. His chest was broad and chiseled, with each muscle well-defined. A dark sprinkle of chest hair trailed down to his stomach. Her gaze followed the line of it down, but before she could reach for his belt, he reached for her wrist and tugged her to him. She slammed into his chest, her nipples pressing against the firm, tan skin she'd just been admiring.

His mouth found hers again and then traveled down her throat. He nipped at her skin with his teeth, soothing it with his lips and tongue. Wade buried his hands in her hair, rubbing the strands between his fingertips. She closed her eyes and just focused on the sensations he coaxed.

Wade's hand slid down her back, caressed a round cheek through the lace of her panties, then continued along the back of her thigh. He tugged her leg up around his hip, then wrapped his arm around her waist. With his mouth still on her throat, he lifted her off the ground, hooking her other leg around him.

Clinging to his shoulders, Tori squealed at the sudden movement. Then with a laugh she threw her head back, arching her spine and offering her breasts to him. He accepted, taking one nipple into his mouth as he walked them slowly through the large open room. The tug of pleasure shot straight to her center, and Tori groaned loudly. She thought she remembered him saying his brothers had left, but she didn't know that for sure. She hoped no one else was here, but frankly she didn't care. She needed him now.

"Bed?" she whispered.

His lips parted with her flesh only long enough to say, "Upstairs."

Tori glanced at the staircase behind them. They'd been moving toward it since he picked her up. He began to carry her up the stairs, but she shook her head. "Too far," she gasped between ragged breaths. "Right here."

"On the stairs?"

"Yes, now."

Wade didn't argue. He eased her onto one of the steps, the plush carpeting meeting her bare skin. She leaned back onto her elbows, sprawled across the steps as he pulled away to look at her. His breath was rapid, his chest rising and falling as if he'd been running a marathon. His gaze slowly traveled up her body until it met her eyes. The green depths were almost penetrating.

He didn't look away as he unfastened his belt and eased down his own pants and briefs. Tori caught only a quick glance of his magnificent body and the flash of foil in his palm before he was crouched down, kneeling on a step between her leather-wrapped ankles. He lifted one leg and planted a kiss on her ankle, then on her inner calf and knee. He placed a searing kiss on her inner thigh just above the lace band of her stocking. Tori's leg quivered in his hands, his hot breath near torture on her exposed center. His fingertips glided across her panties, hooking around the edge before tugging them down her legs and tossing them to the bottom step.

Tori let out a heavy sigh as his body moved back up to cover her own. His blazing-hot skin glided deliciously across hers. The man was as hot-blooded as they came, like a furnace. He picked up where he'd left off, placing a kiss on her hip bone, then on her belly. The evening stubble on his chin scratched and tickled her delicate skin. His mouth moved over her stomach to the valley between her breasts. Braced on his elbows, he took his time teasing each nipple into fierce, throbbing peaks with his tongue.

She could feel the brush of his arousal along her inner thigh. Her whole body ached to have him inside her, but Wade didn't appear to be in the same hurry she was. "Wade, please," she said, her hands tugging impatiently on his upper arms.

He pulled away for just a moment, quickly sheathing

himself in latex and moving back between her thighs.
This time he covered her completely, and she was glad.
She'd quickly become accustomed to his warmth, and
losing it, even for a few moments, had left her shivering. Now that he was back where he belonged, Tori
tilted her head to look him in the eyes. Wade dipped
down to kiss her again. As his tongue slowly penetrated
her, so did the rest of him. He surged forward. Inch by
inch he filled her. Tori held her breath and eased her
legs open farther to accept all of him.

When at last he was buried deep inside her, Wade
stilled. His lips parted from hers so he could suck in
a ragged breath. "Victoria," he murmured against her
lips, "you feel so incredible."

His words were nearly as sexy as the almost pained
expression on his face as he said them. Tori drew her
stocking-clad legs up and wrapped them around his
waist. That movement alone was enough to draw a hiss
from his lips. She placed a hand on each side of his face.
Feeling the rough stubble in her palms, she drew him
down for another soft, brief kiss. "Love me," she said.

A flash of challenge lit in his eyes. Pulling back, he
thrust into her again without breaking their visual connection. This time it was Tori who cried out. Before
she could recover, he moved again and again. The desire that had been building inside her for the past few
hours was now a constant throb of pleasure. The ache
of it increased with their every movement.

Everything else faded away but that feeling. There
was no land to be bought. No lost job. No animosity
between them. Not even the burn of the rug on their elbows or the bite of the stair across her back registered.
There was only their frenzied drive to fulfill the need.

Tori clung to him, panting and whispering words of

encouragement in his ear. "Yes," she repeated, the pressure building inside reaching the critical point. "Yes, Wade, yes!" Tori cried out as the wave of her climax crashed over her. Her body trembled against his as he quickened his pace and found his own release. The roar was almost deafening as he poured everything he had into her, then collapsed.

Tori held him to her, the sweat of their bare skin mingling together, until their rapid breaths finally slowed. It was only then, when the passionate fog had lifted, that she could find the strength to speak again.

"Let's go find a real bed," she said.

Wade woke up to the delicious smell of coffee and bacon. He smiled, shifted and rolled over, expecting to see the other side of the bed empty. Instead he found himself looking at Tori's bare back.

Molly.

Wade flopped back against his pillows in disgust. The movement was enough to wake Tori. She tugged the sheets modestly over her breasts and sat up, a touch disoriented. When she turned to look at Wade, he was struck by how beautiful she looked, tousled. Her red hair was wild, her lips swollen from a night of kisses. She looked like a woman who had been thoroughly and completely loved the night before.

And he'd be inclined to pick up where they left off if he didn't think his mother was downstairs.

"Good morning," he said.

"Morning," she said with a yawn and a long, feline stretch that accentuated the bare curve of her back. Then her delicate nose wrinkled and her brow furrowed. "Are you cooking something?" she asked.

"No."

"But I—" Tori brought her hand up to her mouth. "Molly isn't downstairs, is she? My panties are…" She lifted the sheet, then quickly brought it back down. "Oh, no. They're still on the stairs."

Wade sat up and shook his head. "Don't worry about all that. I'm not a teenager anymore. And if I know my mother, she's probably pleased as punch to find our clothes strewn across the living room. She knew I was taking you out to dinner last night."

"Are you sure she won't be upset?"

"Extremely. The woman hung mistletoe. She knows exactly what she's doing."

"And what's that?"

Wade swallowed hard and swung his legs out over the edge of the bed. "Working on grandchildren."

He pulled on a pair of his pajama pants from his luggage, turning his back to Tori to hide the laugh her wide, panicked eyes brought on.

"I, uh, I—I mean…"

"Relax. I'm sure the next generation of Edens has yet to be spawned. I'll go run her off."

Wade opened the bedroom door and slipped down the stairs to the ground floor. His mother was nowhere to be found, but she'd certainly been in the bunkhouse. Their clothes from the living room floor—not the panties, thankfully—had been picked up and neatly laid over the arm of the couch. The coffeepot was on and dripping the last of a fresh pot. There was a pitcher of orange juice and a foil-wrapped casserole dish on the counter. In the center of the breakfast table was a vase filled with some of the greenhouse-grown roses left over from the pine centerpieces she sold in the shop.

"Is it safe?"

Wade turned to find Tori standing a few steps from

the bottom of the staircase, a blanket wrapped around her like a toga.

"Yes, she's gone. She brought us breakfast."

Tori stooped down at the bottom of the stairs, snatching up her panties. She found her purse by the front door and stuffed the panties inside to hide the evidence in case someone came back. "Breakfast?"

"Yes, are you hungry?"

She smiled sheepishly. "After the meal last night I thought I might never eat again. But I did manage to work up quite an appetite."

That was for sure. After they made it upstairs, they'd taken a shower together, starting another round of love-making they finished in the bed.

"Would you like coffee or orange juice?"

"Juice," she said, reaching for her red dress. "This seems like a little much for breakfast, but I didn't plan for an overnight trip."

"Upstairs in the bedroom drawer are some shirts you're welcome to try on. They'll be big, but it's better than a cocktail dress. And under the sink are some extra toiletries that Molly keeps here in case one of us forgets something. There should be a new toothbrush and anything else you might need."

Tori nodded and slunk back toward the stairs. "That's great. I'll be right back."

By the time she came back downstairs in an oversize Yale alumni sweatshirt, Wade had made them both a plate with breakfast casserole and diced fruit that Molly had left in the fridge. He handed her a glass of orange juice as she sat down at the table.

"This looks wonderful. Molly really didn't have to go to all this trouble."

Wade sat down with a mug of coffee and shook his head. "She lives for this. Don't let her fool you."

Tori took a few bites, quietly eating and avoiding making eye contact with Wade. He wasn't sure if the typical morning after had been made more awkward, or less, by his mother's culinary interference.

"How are you this morning?" he asked.

Tori brushed her loose hair behind her ear and took a sip of juice before she answered. "Honestly, I'm a little weirded out that your mother knows we slept together, and I'm still trying to process that fact myself."

"Do you regret last night?"

"No," she said. "But sex always changes things. I'm not quite sure what's going to happen from here."

"I believe we go out on another date."

Tori frowned. "I don't know if I'm ready for that. Three dates in a week. With a man who wants my land and fired me from my first real job."

"That still bothers you, doesn't it?"

"Yes," she admitted. "Despite what you believe, I didn't do anything wrong. I didn't so much as shake that guy's hand, much less handle anything else. I was so naive. And when you fired me, it felt like I'd lost everything. My apartment, my confidence in my abilities. Even a little of my trust in men."

Now it was Wade's turn to frown. "I damaged your ability to trust men?"

Tori shrugged. "In a way. More me not being able to trust that I know what I'm doing in a relationship. I had been attracted to you. You were the boss, and I knew it was a bad idea, but I couldn't help it. Sometimes I wondered if the feeling was mutual. Those couple of nights that we worked late together, I thought I'd felt a spark of something."

"You did. I wanted very badly to ask you out, but I wasn't sure if it would be appropriate, since you worked for me."

Tori sighed and sat back in her chair. "I'm glad I didn't imagine that. One afternoon I remember asking your assistant, Lauren, what she thought, since I figured she knew you best. She said I was way off. That I wasn't your type at all. Then you fired me, and I figured I must've been imagining things."

Hearing the name of his former admin was like finding a missing piece to an old mental puzzle. "Lauren," he said.

"Yes. What about her?"

"What else did she tell you about me and my tastes?"

Tori paused for a second and turned to look at him. "You don't think…?"

"She made it all up," he said with certainty. Something about Tori's ethics violation had always troubled him, but he could never put his finger on what, aside from him not wanting to believe she could do it. There had been a real connection between them. That was probably why the idea of her with another man was more painful than it should've been. "Lauren is the one who told me she saw you having an intimate dinner with one of our suppliers. The next day you started making recommendations… The timing was too suspicious."

"He had a superior product. He didn't have to seduce me for an endorsement. But why would she say that about me when it wasn't true?"

With that piece in place, the entire picture became painfully clear. "I am so sorry," he said, shaking his head. "This was all my fault."

"How? If Lauren did it, why are you to blame?"

Wade had ended up firing Lauren only a few months after Tori. She'd seemed sweet at first. After Tori left, she developed some extremely suggestive behaviors. She made it no secret she wanted Wade, although he wasn't interested at all. After catching her being rude on the phone to Julianne, thinking she was a girlfriend and not his sister, he had to let her go. She was an efficient employee, but she was letting a misplaced territoriality compromise her performance.

"She must've been jealous of you. I don't know why I didn't connect this before. I asked her one afternoon if she could help me find out what kind of flowers you liked. I was going to send some to your home and ask if you'd like to have dinner."

"I never got any flowers," Tori replied.

"I never got to send them. Lauren showed up with her story about you the next day. It never occurred to me that she was jealous enough of you to sabotage your whole career like that, but that has to be it. Not long after you left, Lauren made it quite obvious that she was interested in me. I'm sorry I didn't believe you."

Tori nodded and glanced down at the remains of her breakfast. "There was no way to prove it either way. You did what you had to do."

"I feel horrible. I want to make it up to you somehow."

"That's not necessary," she said. "I know I've given you a lot of grief over it, but look at where I am now. It might have been a rocky transition, but things turned out the way they were meant to. If I had continued to work for you, I'd probably still be there, making you money, but I never would've gone for my dream. When I lost my job, I took the chance to start my own company, and it was the best thing I could've done. When

I think of it that way, I don't know…maybe I should be thanking you."

"Yet you've been angry with me all this time?"

"I was hurt because you didn't believe me. It was easy to blame you for the upheaval in my life that came after it. The truth is probably that I wasn't ready to settle down in one place yet. I was just rebelling from my parents. Who knows, if you hadn't fired me, I might've quit a few weeks later and started wandering again."

"What made you ready to settle down now? Here?"

"I started doing genealogy a few years back as a way to connect with my roots. My parents were so nomadic I never really met any extended family or knew where we came from. A little digging uncovered that my father's family was from this area, a few generations back. Cornwall was where they settled after migrating to America from Ireland."

She took a sip of juice before continuing. "I came up here on a whim once, when I had a free weekend away from the project in Philadelphia. I just drove around, mostly. But then I spied this beautiful wooded area and I pulled over and started walking around. For the first time in my life, I felt like I was home. Like I'd spiritually dropped anchor. I wanted to stay here. So I started looking for land to buy. I couldn't have found a more perfect piece of property than the one your parents were offering. I snatched it up and started hatching plans to build my dream house."

Seeing the excitement light up Tori's face, Wade felt smacked in the gut with guilt. She longed for a connection to her family and a chance to build a real home. And he wanted her to. He felt crappy for keeping her from that dream. But he couldn't risk the body being found, even for her dreams. "And once again, I've charged into your life and tried to ruin it all."

She chuckled softly but didn't contradict him. "Life should never be boring."

Wade watched a touch of sadness creep into her eyes. Sadness that he knew he was partially responsible for. It made him want to sweep her into his arms and kiss her until she was too wrapped up in them to be distressed. He wanted to distract her with something so fantastic she wouldn't think about the past for at least a few days.

"I want to take you to New York."

She looked up, startled by the sudden change in topic. "New York? Why?"

"I want to make amends for the past and take you someplace as exciting and beautiful as you are. I want to spend New Year's Eve with you in Times Square."

"Are you kidding me?" She laughed. "I'd pretty much prefer to be anywhere over freezing to death in a mad crush of people in Times Square. I'll be happy to watch the ball drop via my television, though thank you for asking me."

Wade smiled and reached across the table to take her hand. "We're going to New York. Pack your bags because I'm picking you up Monday morning. We're going to see a show. We're going to eat some great food. And when that ball drops, you and I are going to be right there to watch it."

Tori squirmed but didn't pull away. "I don't know, Wade. As nice as that sounds, I don't want to spend my night outside in the cold with a million other people. I'd rather spend it alone with you."

Wade smiled; a plan was forming in his head that would satisfy both their desires. "Who said anything about being outside?"

Eight

"Oh. My. Dear. Lord."

Wade tipped the bellhop and followed Tori's voice into the penthouse suite's master bedroom. He found her standing in front of the wall of windows that lined the room from floor to ceiling. The view overlooked Times Square and the hustle and bustle of the theater district. He'd had this exact view in mind when he renovated this building. His architect had designed this suite, and these windows, for the precise experience Wade had planned for tonight.

"This is amazing. You can see everything from here. How did you get us a room like this on such short notice?"

"Easy," he said, sneaking up behind her to wrap his arms around her waist and tug her against him. "I just called and asked for it. Although it helps when you know the owner and renovated the hotel."

"Ah…" she said, curling into his warmth. "I should've known better than to think you'd be down there with the crowds tonight. Look how many people are already standing around and there's hours to go."

"I've done that before," he said, biting at her earlobe. "When I was younger and poorer. It was fun. But I'd much rather watch the ball drop tonight with your naked body pressed against this glass."

Tori responded by arching her back and pressing her hips into his throbbing desire. He growled against her neck. "And the best part is that these windows are one-way glass."

"Nobody can see in, even at night with the lights on?"

"Correct." Wade's hand snaked across her stomach and up to caress one firm breast through the silky fabric of her blouse. Tori gasped softly when his thumb brushed over the hard peak of her nipple. "No one can see me do this, even if they were right on the other side of the window."

"That should prove interesting," she whispered, near purring.

"Indeed," Wade said, undoing the top button of her shirt. "We have all night to test our theory." He moved down for the second button. Then the doorbell rang.

Blast. He'd ordered room service, hadn't he? It seemed like a good idea at the time. He just hadn't realized how much driving in the car with her would turn him on. Maybe it was the memories of their drive home from the restaurant that had made it hard to focus on the road.…

Tori pulled away, smiling when she saw the pained expression on his face. "Sorry. Are we expecting someone?"

"Dinner."

She arched an eyebrow and breezed past him to the front door of the suite. "You mean you aren't taking me out somewhere?"

"On New Year's Eve? In the theater district? No, sorry. You said you didn't like the crowds, and there's no way to avoid them tonight unless we dine in."

Tori opened the door, and a man rolled in a cart covered in silver domes. He pushed the cart over to the dining room table and transferred the platters, unveiling them one by one. There was lobster, prime rib, herb-roasted potatoes, haricots verts and a platter of plump red strawberries with a bowl of chocolate fondue in the center. Last of all he placed on the table an ice bucket containing a bottle of champagne, and two glasses.

Wade tipped the server. The man thanked him before disappearing just as quickly as he'd arrived.

"This is quite a spread you've ordered. You've done nothing but feed me indulgent food since we met."

"Nothing?" he asked with a mischievous grin.

"Okay, well, it's not all you've done, but we certainly haven't worked off all these calories, either. I'm going to grow out of my clothes."

"Well…" Wade approached her and continued undoing the buttons of her blouse where he'd left off. "We'd better remedy that, right away."

By the time they got around to dinner, it was nearly cold, but salvageable. The only warm food remaining was the ramekin of chocolate fondue, which was heated by a candle to keep it fluid for dipping. It didn't matter. Tori had worked up a huge appetite and wasn't feeling very particular.

"The festivities will be starting soon, and the view

in the dining room isn't as grand. How do you feel about a picnic here in the bedroom?" Wade asked as Tori slipped into the bathroom.

"Sounds great. Is it safe to say we're staying in for the night?"

"That was the plan."

"Okay," she called, eyeing her wardrobe bag hanging beside her in the bathroom. Wade hadn't really told her what they were going to be doing, so she'd packed a variety of clothing. Unzipping the bag a few inches, she spied the beaded neckline of the dress she'd been dying to wear.

It was a fully beaded midnight-blue gown with a halter neckline and a slit up the side that went almost to her hip. It had been an impulse purchase. Tori rarely bought things like that because her storage space was at a premium in the Airstream. She'd simply had to own the dress and figured she'd worry later about what she would wear it to. She'd packed it for their trip thinking they might go someplace fancy. But why not wear it tonight?

She was spending New Year's Eve in a glamorous penthouse overlooking Times Square. She was about to dine on lobster and champagne with a handsome date. The dress would be perfectly suited for a night like this if they were in a chic restaurant or at a party in a grand ballroom. It should be just as suitable for a private dinner for two.

With a giggle of girlish excitement, she fully unzipped the bag and slipped into the gown. The indulgent purchase had been sealed the moment she'd first tried it on. It fitted as though it were made just for her, hugging each curve. Tori reapplied her lipstick, ran her fingers through her hair and went back into the bedroom.

Wade had carried the food into the master bedroom and spread out a blanket for a picnic on the floor by the window. He had slipped back into his trousers but left off the dress shirt. It was thrown across a chair in the living room the last time she saw it, but Tori was glad he'd left it off. Wade had a magnificent chest, and she couldn't spend enough time admiring the hard lines and the dark curls of his chest hair. Unfortunately she hadn't found a reason for him to just stay shirtless all the time.

He was kneeling on the blanket, pouring flutes of champagne, when he looked up at her—and froze. His jaw fell open, and his gaze took in every inch of her body. He licked his lips before he spoke. "You did hear me say we were staying in, right?"

"Yes," she said with a smile. "But I felt like dressing up a little bit for the occasion." Tori held out her arms and spun around for effect. "Do you like it?"

He swallowed hard. "Very much."

"Is it too much for a picnic on the floor?"

"Not at all." He reached out his hand and helped her down onto the blanket. "Looking that beautiful, you can do whatever the hell you like."

Tori blushed. She felt beautiful in this dress, but hearing him say it made her all the happier that she'd decided to put it on, impractical as it was. She settled down beside him, curling her legs to the side and spreading the gown out around her.

Wade handed her a glass of champagne and held up his own for a toast. "To…letting go of the past and embracing a new year and new beginnings."

It was the perfect toast for them in so many ways. Over the past week it did seem as though they had come so far. There was a time in her life when the mention of his name would've sent her into a rampage. Now, sitting across from him, she felt that everything had changed. Thoughts of Wade brought on tingly, warm sensations and a nervous, excited feeling in her stomach.

Tori clinked her glass flute to his. "To new beginnings," she echoed. And that was really what she wanted. A fresh start. Knowing the truth about the circumstances around her firing made the past, the past. She could finally set down the grudge she'd held all these years, and she was glad. She didn't want that dark cloud hanging over their relationship.

Relationship.

Is that what this had become? Things had moved so quickly, but it certainly felt like something more than a fling. But a relationship required more than just attraction and compatibility. It also required trust. She wasn't sure that she had much left. Wade had damaged it pretty badly. Whatever ability she'd regained after several years had been shattered by Ryan. Was trusting a man even possible? And trusting a man like Wade Mitchell? That seemed out of the question. Even with their past resolved, he still wanted her property. That hadn't changed.

Taking a sip of her champagne, she realized how badly she wanted to trust him. This had started out as a game between them. A battle of wills to see who would crack under pleasure, so to speak. But now…she feared it was her. Wade seemed as though he'd put the game behind them, as she had, but she couldn't know for sure. She wanted something more between them. Tori wanted to build her dream house. And if she was honest with herself, she wanted Wade living in it with her.

The thought made her champagne hard to swallow.

How had she made that kind of leap in just a few short days? Maybe it wasn't much of a leap. She'd wanted him years ago. Fantasized about more. Perhaps that was why his supposed betrayal hurt her so badly. The feelings had remained, buried under her anger and rushing to the surface the moment the barricades were brushed away.

"I'm starving," Wade said, oblivious to the thoughts running through her mind.

She forced the champagne down her throat to respond. "Me, too." Better for her to focus on food than on her dangerous thoughts.

Wade made them both plates, and they sat eating quietly. They'd spent so much time together in the car on the drive down that they were clearly out of small talk. That left only serious discussions. She wasn't sure either of them was ready for that.

Tori was biting into a chocolate-coated strawberry when Wade set aside his plate and looked down at his watch. "It's getting close to midnight," he said. "We don't want to miss it. I'll pour more champagne."

Tori nodded and accepted his hand to stand up. She went to the window. The dim lights in the bedroom suite allowed her to see everything outside. The lights and activity in the square were stunning. It was amazing that so many people could be in one place at one time. Crowds were gathered around stages where musicians performed for broadcast specials. The sound was probably deafening, yet not a peep made it through to their room. She had seen this scene on television every year, but somehow looking down on it was a completely new experience.

As was the warmth at her bare back as Wade came up behind her. He brought an arm around her to hold out her refilled glass of champagne. On a nearby table, he'd set down the platter of strawberries and chocolate.

His hands gently swept her hair over one shoulder. His lips seared a trail across her bare skin, sending a shiver of anticipation down her spine. It didn't matter how many times she'd had him, she wanted more. Her need almost seemed to get worse, like an escalating addiction. Her body reacted in an instant to his touch. Her breasts tightened within the confines of her gown. Her belly clenched with need.

Wade's fingertips sought out the clasp of her dress at her neck. With a snap it came undone. The fabric slipped over her skin, gliding to the ground with the heavy thump of beads. Tori kicked the dress aside and placed her drink on the table with the fruit. He followed suit, obviously needing both of his hands for what he had planned.

Grasping her by the waist, he turned her to face him. "We've still got a few minutes," he said. "Plenty of time for some dessert."

Without his powerful green gaze leaving hers, he plucked a strawberry from the platter and dipped it in chocolate. He held the fruit in front of her lips, but before she could bite into it, he dropped it to her collarbone. He dragged the berry down her throat to the hollow between her breasts. It left a warm trail of chocolate in its wake. The plump, red fruit circled one breast, teasing at her aching nipple, then traveled to the other. Nearly devoid of chocolate now, the strawberry made its way back to her lips.

She took a bite, the sweet juice instantly filling her mouth. Tori chewed and swallowed as Wade patiently held the rest of the berry for her to finish it. "Don't you want any?" she asked.

"No," he said with a wicked grin. "I prefer the chocolate." Wade set the rest of the berry aside and leaned in to kiss her. His lips tasted of champagne. He buried his fingers in her hair and moaned against her mouth. Tori drank him in, feeling a touch light-headed from his kisses and the alcohol.

When he did pull away, it was to clean up the mess he'd made. He bent Tori back over his arm, and she offered up her throat and breasts to him. He started with her neck, tasting and teasing her with his tongue as he licked every drop of chocolate from her skin. The scalding heat of his lips moved down her chest, following the berry's path to curl around each breast. He bathed each nipple, coaxing it into painfully hard peaks, then biting gently until she cried out.

By now, Tori was certain the chocolate was long gone, but Wade was nothing if not thorough. He traveled back up to her lips and murmured against them, "It's almost time. I don't want you to miss seeing it."

He spun Tori in his arms until she was facing the window and the chaotic scene below. She felt oddly exposed, standing completely naked in front of the glass. It was an exhilarating feeling. Dangerous, yet safe, since no one could see her. Firm hands pressed at her back until she bent forward and braced her hands against the glass. Wade's palm glided leisurely down her spine. He gripped her hips, tugging her bottom back against his hard desire.

"One minute to go. Let's see if you can last that long." Wade sought out her moist center with his fingers. They glided expertly over her, coaxing the building tension of release deep inside.

Tori's fingers clutched uselessly at the glass, but it was all she could do. In front of her there was nothing but the lights of the cityscape, as though they were making love on the roof. She gasped as a finger penetrated her, her muscles tightening around him. A wave of pleasure rocked her, but it wasn't enough. "Wade," she said, an edge of desperation creeping into her voice.

"Fifteen seconds." He leaned over her and placed a burning kiss between her shoulder blades.

Tori glanced over her shoulder and saw him kick aside his trousers. Soon. Thank goodness. She needed him now. All of him. "Ten, nine, eight," she whispered as the numbers began counting down, the building pressure of her orgasm certain to beat the clock. "Seven, six, five."

His fingers glided over her moist flesh, taking her closer to the edge. "Four, three, two, one," Wade said, thrusting inside her at the stroke of midnight.

The infamous ball dropped to the base, the number of the New Year lighting up, but Tori hardly gave it a glance before closing her eyes and absorbing the pleasurable impact on her body. He barely moved in her before she came undone. As the cheers and shouts rang out in the city below, Tori heard only her own cries.

Wade filled her, pushed her, thrilled her and touched her as no man ever had before. He took her to a place she hadn't known existed, and she wanted to stay there with him in this moment forever.

"Oh, Wade," she gasped as the last throbs of pleasure dissipated.

Wade's arms snaked around her waist, tugging her up until her bare back pressed against his chest. "I could make love to you all night and never have enough."

"There's quite a few hours left," she teased, breathless.

"Is that a challenge?" he asked, thrusting hard into her.

Tori laughed and tightened her muscles around him. "Absolutely."

In one quick move Wade pulled away and swept Tori up into his arms. She squealed in surprise, but before she could recover, he dropped her, bouncing, to the bed.

He was back over her in an instant, driving into her body with renewed fervor. The laughter died in her throat as the pleasure began coursing through her veins once again. This time when her release came, so did his. He groaned low against her neck and lost himself inside her body.

Tori cradled him against her as his trembling arms and legs threatened to give way beneath him. After he caught his breath, she tipped his chin up so he could look at her. There was a green fire blazing in his eyes, and she was pleased she was responsible for it. She brought her lips to his, this kiss tender and meaningful.

"Happy New Year, Wade."

The rest of the champagne was forgotten, the strawberries abandoned. Wade didn't care. He had his redhaired beauty in his arms, and that was all he wanted. For the first time in months—hell, years—Wade felt at peace. It was possible that he'd never felt like this. The world was stable on its axis. Tori had done that. The woman whose spirit he had been determined to crush so he could get what he wanted.

Now, with her head resting on his chest and the flaming silk of her hair sprawled over her shoulders and his stomach, he knew he couldn't go through with it. His plan to seduce her had backfired.

The implications were dire. It made him almost sick to his stomach to think of what it might mean for his family. If the body was ever uncovered, it would ruin everything. But that was his mistake. His price to pay. Not Tori's.

There had to be another way. He'd figure something out. He always did.

"Wade, are you still awake?"

"Yes."

Tori rolled off his chest and looked at him. "What was this trip about, really?"

Wade frowned. "What do you mean?"

"The hotel, the food, the champagne—that's a lot of effort just to make up for the whole job thing."

He supposed it might seem that way, but he didn't mind. Having money and powerful connections allowed him the luxury of doing things for people when he wanted to. "You're worth the effort."

"You are, too, you know."

Wade had the sudden urge to climb out of bed and go get a drink, but Tori had her arms clasped around him like steel manacles. He swallowed hard. "You're just supposed to say thank you."

"Thank you." Tori held him in place with her icy blue eyes. "What happened to you, Wade?"

He knew what she meant without her elaborating. He was surprised. Few people ever bothered to ask him about his life before the Edens, so he didn't tell the story very often. Those who mattered in his life already knew. Except Tori. She mattered. More than he ever wanted or expected her to.

"A person doesn't become such an overachiever, so driven to prove himself, without a reason," she pressed. "You don't have to do things to impress me. I don't need ten-course French dinners and penthouses in Manhattan to want to spend time with you. What are you trying to prove? And to whom?"

With a sigh Wade let his head drop back against the

pillows. If he had to talk about it, at least it was dark and he didn't have to look at her. "For a long time I thought I was trying to be a good son for the Edens. To repay them for taking me in and helping me turn my life around. All the good it did me, since they wouldn't accept my money when I tried to give it to them. Then I wondered if maybe I wasn't trying to prove to…those who left…that I was worth keeping."

"Like your mother?"

"Yes. And others. My mother was still in high school when she got pregnant. I wasn't exactly part of her plans. So, after she had me, she played at being a mom for a while. When that didn't work out, she took me over to her aunt's house. What was supposed to be a couple hours of babysitting turned into seven years. She just never came back."

Wade could hear Tori's breath catch in her throat. He didn't want her pity. That was why he never told anyone about this. He'd rather people saw him as the strong, powerful businessman. That was the point, wasn't it? To keep this part hidden? And yet he wanted to tell her everything now that he'd started talking. He wanted to let Tori in.

"My aunt never married and wasn't particularly interested in having children, but it wasn't bad with her. I didn't know any different. When she died of breast cancer and my mother was still off the grid, I ended up in the foster system. She had never terminated her parental rights, so I couldn't be adopted even if someone had wanted to. I doubt anyone but the Edens would have. I bounced around a lot. I was an angry child. Rebellious. A trouble starter. I had a lot of crap to work through for a ten-year-old, but it was how I coped. I guess it was easier to push people away than to get close to someone who would eventually cast me aside. But the Edens didn't fall for that game. They wouldn't let me push them away. They believed in me. So I changed my tactic to be the best man I could possibly be."

"And now you're successful, powerful and have a family that loves you."

"And you know what that got me?" he said, a bitter edge creeping into his voice.

"What?"

"A mother showing up on my doorstep with her hand out."

"What did you do?"

"Well, as you said, I'm always out to prove myself, so I did what I felt I should. I gave her a lump sum of cash and bought her a house as far from New York as I could get—in San Diego. And I made her sign a contract agreeing to never contact me or anyone in my family again, or she'd have to repay me for everything."

Tori's grip on him tightened ever so slightly. "And she agreed to that?"

Wade had not been there for the contract negotiation, but his lawyer told him she couldn't sign fast enough. There was a part of him that had hoped she wouldn't. That she had changed and wanted to get to know the son she'd abandoned. He'd been a fool for even entertaining that fantasy. "Without hesitating. So in the end, my money and my success didn't prove anything to anyone."

"What about to yourself?"

Especially not to himself. No one else on earth was able to see inside him and know what he was truly like the way he could. Strip away the money and the suits and what was he left with? When things were important, truly important, he failed.

He couldn't protect his family the way he should have. If he had done his job, Heath never would've had to do what no thirteen-year-old boy should have to do. Julianne wouldn't have to carry those dark memories with her. His parents wouldn't be secretly selling off pieces of the farm to stay afloat. No success in business could make up for that kind of personal failure.

"Is that even possible?" he asked. "Can someone like me ever reach the point where they've achieved enough? How would I know when I've expunged my sins? There's always the opportunity to disappoint myself. Or someone else."

"You haven't disappointed me."

Wade chuckled. "I haven't, now? Well, considering I fired you erroneously, harassed you mercilessly and want to take your land away from you, I imagine you have very low standards."

Tori sat up on one elbow and looked down at him. "I don't have low standards. I think I'm just better at seeing past the bull."

"And where did you learn that skill? Traipsing across America studying the human condition?"

"Something like that," she admitted. "Attending the school of life has its perks and its pitfalls. I think never building real relationships handicapped me when I grew older. I was too trusting because I'd never had the opportunity to be hurt. I didn't build relationships, like you, but because I couldn't. We were gone too quickly. I was naive."

"You?"

"Yes." She smiled. "I wasn't always so cynical. The

real world brought that. What life didn't teach me, my ex-boyfriend did."

She hadn't mentioned much about her past relationships, but Wade picked up on the pained tone in her voice. The darkness couldn't veil that. "What did he do?"

Tori sighed and shrugged. "Like I said, I was too trusting. He took advantage of the fact that I was always moving. I wasn't going to pressure him for marriage or a commitment, even after years together, because I wasn't in that place."

Wade could tell where this was going. "He was married."

"With three kids. Living happily outside Boston. When I told him I was thinking of buying land in Connecticut, he came unglued."

"And that was the last man you dated?"

Tori nodded.

Wade already felt like crap for the way things had gone down between him and Tori. Knowing she was trying to recover her trust in men when he showed up, scheming to manipulate her, made it that much worse. She deserved more than just a luxurious weekend in Manhattan. She deserved a week in Paris. Or better yet, for him to go away and leave her life and her plans alone.

"Tori," he started, not quite sure at first what he was going to say. "I'm sorry."

"For what?"

Wade swallowed the lump in his throat. He had so many feelings swirling in his gut. So many things he wanted to say to her. But he couldn't put them into words. Wouldn't. At least not until after he'd dealt with the situation that had brought him here in the first place. Whether he intended it or not, Tori could get hurt. And he didn't want to say or do anything now that might make the pain that much sharper.

"For everything," he whispered.

Nine

Tori strolled into Daisy's Diner a few days later with a bounce in her step and a smile on her face that wouldn't fade away. Her trip to New York with Wade had been wonderful. Magical. Romantic. Everything she'd hoped for and more than she'd dreamed it could be. They'd strolled through the city, window-shopping and sightseeing. They went to a show. They talked and spent hours in each other's arms. And then it was time to come home.

Back to Connecticut—and reality. She hadn't seen Wade since they'd returned to Cornwall. They both had things to do. She was certain he would have to return to his life in Manhattan soon, although he hadn't mentioned it and she hadn't asked. He had a business to run. And she had a house to build. But they'd opted to meet here tonight for dinner.

"Hey, there," Rose said as Tori walked past her usual seat. "No counter service today?"

"No." She smiled. "I have a date tonight, so I thought a booth might be better."

"Oh, really." Rose poured a mug of hot water for Tori's tea and came out from behind the counter with two menus tucked under her arm. She sat across from Tori in the corner booth she'd selected. "Spill it," she demanded, pushing the hot water over to her customer.

Tori began fidgeting with the mug, knowing her cheeks were probably as red as her hair now. "Wade is meeting me here."

"Wade Mitchell? The man who was making you crazy a week ago?"

"The same."

Rose flung her dark ponytail back over her shoulder and leaned in closer. "So, you wanna tell me what happened between then and now?"

Tori could barely explain it. Everything had changed. Even the past, if that were possible. "It feels like the world has shifted."

Rose sat back against the padded pleather of the booth, her brown eyes wide. "You're in love with him."

"What?" Tori perked up at her friend's bold assessment. "No, no. That's silly. It's only been a few days."

Rose crossed her arms over her chest and refused to budge on the subject. "I can assure you, with the Eden boys, a few days is all it takes."

The words were like a fist to her gut. The truth barreling into her at fifty miles an hour. She was in love with him.

"I...I like him a lot," she countered, even as her mind raced with a different version of the facts. "We have a good time together. But it's nothing more than that. He's leaving to go home shortly, so it would be stupid of me to go and fall in love with him."

Rose nodded mechanically, clearly disbelieving every word of Tori's argument. Tori understood. She didn't believe her own words, either. And they were sensible. She shouldn't be in love with Wade. He *was* leaving. They *weren't* serious. She couldn't trust him because he still wanted her land. None of that added up to a fairy-tale romance. Just another disaster waiting to happen like before.

She wished someone would tell her heart that.

The heart in question started pounding madly in her chest when she looked up and spied Wade coming in the entrance. "He's here," she whispered.

Rose dutifully got up and flashed a smile to Wade on her way back to the counter. "What can I get you to drink tonight?"

"Coffee, thanks," Wade said. "It's freezing out there." He slipped out of his jacket and tossed it into the booth before sliding in where Rose had been sitting.

Wade looked so handsome tonight. He was wearing a dark blue collared shirt with thin gray pinstripes. His skin was freshly shaved and slightly pink from the sting of the icy wind outside. Tori wanted to reach out and touch his face. She wanted to breathe in his cologne. Some of her clothing had come home smelling like him after their trip. She hadn't been able to make herself go to the Laundromat to wash them yet.

Tori suddenly felt like a shy, smitten teenager sitting with him. Her realization of love only a minute before left her feeling vulnerable even though there was no way he could know how she felt. She certainly wasn't about to tell him. She had barely come to terms with it herself, although sitting on the edge of her bed sniffing a sweater should've been her first clue.

"How are you?" he asked.

Tori smiled, although it felt nervous and forced to her. She hoped it didn't look that way. "Good. You?"

"Good," he said. Wade looked down at the menu and began thoroughly studying it without elaborating.

Tori winced and hid her face with her own menu. Did he notice? Things felt weird when they'd never felt weird before. It was all her doing. She needed to act normal. This was the same man she'd spent a good part of the past week with. Naked. After that, dinner in the local restaurant should be no big deal. She just had to relax.

Rose came back with the coffee; she took their orders and the menus. Now neither of them had anything to hide behind. Once Rose disappeared into the kitchen, Tori took a deep breath. "I had a nice time in New York. Thank you for taking me. You know you didn't have to go to that much trouble."

"No trouble at all. I had a great time, too. I'm glad we were able to go. It was certainly more exciting than spending New Year's Eve here with my folks. They never even make it up to midnight. As kids, we used to stay up in the bunkhouse and watch Dick Clark on television after they went to bed."

"It must be strange to stay up here this long without the others. Are you heading back to New York soon?" Tori almost didn't want to know how much time she had left, but she had to ask.

Wade nodded. "In a couple days. I still have a few things to take care of before I go back."

"That's right. You still haven't bought my land," she said with a weak smile. She'd enjoyed the past few days without the topic coming up. "Time is a-ticking on that."

He glanced down at his mug and took a sip. "I guess I'm not going to worry too much about that anymore."

Tori's brow shot up in surprise. She didn't hide it well at all. "What?"

"You don't want to sell it to me. I can't make you. I don't know what I could offer to change your mind, so there's no point in fighting over it anymore."

What should've been a victorious moment didn't feel quite how she'd expected. Going up against Wade, she'd always secretly thought she would lose. One way or another he would wear her down. And now, although he'd named her the victor, it didn't seem as if she'd won. After the past few days, a part of her didn't want to beat him. The thought had crossed Tori's mind that if he'd stay, she'd consider selling it to him. She wanted to build a home, not just a house. Somehow having Wade there with her was an integral piece of her design.

Selling him the land would make him happy. She wanted him to be happy. She could find another piece of land, but replacing Wade's place in her heart felt nearly impossible.

And yet, she felt a tug of hope deep inside. If he no longer wanted her property, maybe she could have both him and the land. She'd known trusting Wade would be an issue as long as he had this ulterior motive. If that was gone, what could that mean? Had he really given up wanting the land or did he care too much about her to hurt her like that? He hadn't said anything about how he felt for her. If he was going back to New York and life as usual, he probably felt nothing at all but had just run out of time.

She'd be left with no reason to hate him when it was all over.

"I'd like to spend the last few days with you before I go."

She hadn't expected that at all. If he wasn't just romancing the property away from her, maybe there was more here than she'd thought. With a sigh of dismay, Tori shook her head. Wade always seemed to want the things she couldn't give. "I have to leave tomorrow. I'm going to Philadelphia for a few days. They're having the ribbon-cutting ceremony on my building down there on Saturday afternoon. I've got to wrap up all the loose ends. I probably won't be back until the seventh or eighth."

"Oh." Wade's expression was curious. A hint of disappointment mixed in with something else she couldn't put her finger on. She could almost see his mind spinning. She remembered that expression from watching him at his desk when she worked with him.

"You could come with me," she suggested.

He looked at her and shook his head. "I can't. I'll need to be back in Manhattan before that."

"I guess I'll have to catch up with you in the city sometime. Or the next time you're up this way."

Wade nodded, his expression guarded. He must've realized, as she had, that this would be their last date. Their last night together. "Do you have another project coming up that you'll be traveling to soon?"

"Not for a few months. I'm going to Vermont for a while this summer to design a ski lodge. Until then, I'll be here, working on building my house."

"Do you have the final plans drawn up yet?"

Yes and no. She had twenty plans completed, but for some reason her clarity about what she wanted had become muddled over the holidays. "I have to make a few final decisions. That's all. I should be able to get the contractors in place to break ground in the next few weeks."

Wade's green eyes widened just a touch at her words, but Rose brought their plates and the expression vanished. "I should give you Troy Caldwell's number. He's got a great building team that does excellent work."

Tori nodded and tried to focus on her food. She'd heard Caldwell was the guy to work with around here. She just hadn't gotten around to speaking with him before the holidays. It seemed that once she got back from Philadelphia, she'd have plenty of time. Wade would be long gone.

The rest of the meal was spent discussing the neutral topics of local electricians and concrete companies. Every now and again Tori would look up to find Wade watching her. There was a hesitation in his voice, a touch of worry lining his eyes. She wasn't certain she was the cause of it, though. He seemed a million miles away tonight. Maybe the stresses of being away from work were distracting him.

Tori was absentmindedly drawing the design for the front of her home across her plate with her fork and leftover ketchup when Wade's voice startled her. It seemed he wasn't the only one distracted this evening.

"Would you like to come back to the bunkhouse for some dessert? Molly baked a really nice chocolate cream cheese Bundt cake this morning."

His words were asking her if she'd like to join him for dessert, but the intensity of his gaze promised more than that. He wanted to have her in his arms one last time before they parted ways.

Tori knew she should say no. It would be so much easier if she just walked away now. She could take her land, her dignity and what was left of her heart back to her Airstream.

Instead, she found herself meeting his gaze and nodding yes. She wasn't quite ready to say goodbye to Wade.

Yet.

They'd spent another incredible night together. He hated to wake her up that morning but knew she had a schedule to keep. He would rather have lain in bed all day with her ear pressed to his heart and her hair strewed across his chest. He had to admit he'd gotten used to having her there when he woke up—grumpy face, wild hair and all.

But he had to.

After they'd reluctantly gotten out of bed, Wade made his way downstairs. Molly hadn't sneaked in with breakfast today, so Wade made coffee and toasted bagels while Tori showered.

They ate quietly together. There was an awkwardness in the air. For all intents and purposes, their relationship was over. They'd had their last date, their last chance to make love and this was their final breakfast.

Unlike other relationships that ended in angry fireworks or bitter barbs, their relationship would die quietly, because it was the practical thing to do. Neither of them really wanted to say goodbye, but neither was willing to say or do anything to change it. This needed to be the end.

When they were finished, he walked her out to her truck. They loitered at the door, so many unspoken things lingering between them. But Wade wouldn't say what he wanted to. Not until he'd finished what he came here for. And to do that, Tori needed to go to

Philadelphia. If he was successful, maybe he'd call her. Or maybe he'd be smart and just let this whole thing go. If she ever found out the truth about his past, it would be over anyway.

But that didn't mean he didn't want one last embrace. He wrapped his arms around Tori, hugging her tight to his chest. She clung just as fiercely to him, letting go only when he pulled away for their last kiss. He pressed his lips to hers, losing himself in the soft feel of her. There was no heat in the kiss. Just…goodbye.

When he stepped back, Tori quickly slipped on her sunglasses and climbed into the truck. He thought he saw the glint of tears in her eyes for a moment, but it could've been the morning sun blinding her.

"Goodbye, Wade," she said, slamming the truck door closed before he could respond. The engine roared to life, and he watched the truck disappear down the road to the highway.

It was over. And he didn't like it at all. But now it was time to put his plan into action.

If there was one thing Wade knew for certain, it was that he could call Heath at any hour, with any number of crazy requests, and his younger brother would be up for it. Brody second-guessed everything. Xander worried about how things might look. But Heath… He was the impulsive brother, and that was exactly what Wade needed. He headed back inside the bunkhouse to get his phone.

"Hey there, big brother," Heath answered. "What's happening?"

"You busy tomorrow?" Wade cut to the chase. His brother knew him well enough not to take offense. Neither of them usually had the time to waste on pleasantries.

"I don't have to be. What do you need?"

"You, a high-quality metal detector and a large plastic tarp."

"What, no shovels?" Heath joked.

"Dad has those. And the backhoe if we need it."

He'd been using the backhoe that day fifteen years ago as part of his chores on the farm. When he needed to bury the body, it seemed like the quickest and easiest thing to use, since he was working alone. No one would think twice about him driving it around the property. But the grave wasn't really that deep. He hadn't taken the time to bury the body seven or eight feet as he should have.

With Heath's help they could probably skip it this time. "We'll definitely need the metal detector. The snow has mostly melted, so it should be easier, but I still have fifteen years working against me on this. You up for an unorthodox treasure hunt?"

"Sure, yeah," Heath said without hesitation. "Whatever we have to do. I mean, hell, it's my ass if this all goes down wrong. You bet I'll help however I can to keep this a secret. I take it the plan to buy the land didn't work out."

"Nope. This is plan B."

Brody would've lectured him about the failure of plan A, but Heath always rolled with the punches. "What's plan B, exactly?"

"Find the body and move it back onto the family land while she's out of town. Can you come up tomorrow?"

"I can. I'll make some calls and dig up a good metal detector tonight, then leave in the morning."

Tori should have felt excited. There were hundreds of people gathered around the new arts-and-sciences center she'd designed. The press was there, snapping pictures and filming pieces for the nightly news. The mayor had personally shaken her hand and told her she'd done a beautiful job. This was huge exposure for her business.

But she wasn't excited. She was…lonely. This was a big moment for her, and she had no one to share it with. She pasted the smile back on her face for the photos and fought the tears that threatened to ruin the moment.

She wanted to share all of this with Wade. She wanted him standing next to her, beaming with pride. And yet he wasn't there. Why? Because of a stupid piece of land.

That's what it had become to her. She had imagined that it would be a magical thing to own a piece of the earth and make her mark on it by building her dream house. But the reality was much different. Even before Wade had shown up and started throwing money around, she'd begun to have her doubts. She'd dug in her heels only because he wanted something she had.

But he'd changed his mind. Wade wasn't going to fight her for it anymore. Why? Maybe for the same reason she no longer wanted to keep it. If this land was the only thing standing between them, he could have it.

The mayor cut the ribbon, and the crowd cheered amid the blinding flash of cameras. The dignitaries stepped back and the front doors were held open for everyone to go inside. There would be folks wandering around all afternoon sipping champagne, eating appetizers and talking about the virtues of green architecture as though they understood it.

As she watched the crowd file in, she knew she should go in with them. Answer questions. Do interviews. But she hadn't felt so desperate to get out of a place in her whole life.

If she left now, she could be home in a few hours. Wade should still be at the farm. And then she could tell him.

Tell him what? That she loved him? That he could have the land because it was nothing but dirt and rock without him in her life? Maybe. If she could work up the nerve.

Turning away from the building, Tori headed for the parking lot and her truck. She had a few hours' drive to figure out what she wanted to say. But she knew she had to go to Wade. Now.

It was probably thirty degrees outside, but Wade was sweating as though it were summertime. They hadn't even started seriously digging yet. That was probably why. They hadn't found what he was looking for so they could start digging. The afternoon had not gone as well as he'd hoped. The snow had melted, revealing a landscape just as confusing as before. No turtle-shaped rocks. No crooked trees like he remembered. Maybe his memory was faulty. Maybe he'd just been a freaked-out kid that night and the whole incident had gotten scrambled in his mind. He wished someone had gone out there with him.

They'd taken to just running the metal detector over every inch of the property. Periodically, they'd get a hit and they'd dig furiously into the frozen ground, only to find an old quarter or a screw. Heath would move on with the metal detector and Wade would stomp the ground back into place. There was another snowstorm in the forecast for tomorrow. By the time Tori returned, the evidence of their search would be buried for a few weeks and hopefully undetectable.

The sun had set not too long ago, and the darkness was making their job even harder than the rock-hard dirt. Heath had turned on the headlight on one of the four-wheelers, and they both carried flashlights, but they were getting discouraged.

"Wade, I don't see any rocks that look like a turtle. Not even if I scrunch my eyes up and look sideways."

"I know." Wade sighed. Maybe this whole plan was a bad idea. Even if they could find the right place, moving a fifteen-year-old corpse couldn't be easy. It's not as if he would be in one piece anymore.

"I'm not getting much with the metal detector. You're sure he still had that ring on when you buried him?"

"Yes." Wade remembered the large gold ring with the black stone in the center. How could he forget it? He'd had an imprint of it punched into his face once. "I remember because I thought about taking it off so no one could identify him. But I didn't know what to do with it. I decided it was better to just leave it on, since he would've taken it with him when he left."

"I guess that was a good idea. We'd never find him without it."

"I'm beginning to think we won't find him even with it." Wade looked across the dark landscape of Tori's property. The rocky ridge where she planned to build the house was off to the back. There was no way he could've buried anything there, even with the back-hoe. Maybe the construction crew that would build her house wouldn't find anything. Maybe, despite his failures, this secret would stay buried.

"Are you sure it's on her plot and not one of the others?" Heath asked.

At this point, Wade couldn't afford to consider that possibility. To know he'd wasted all this time on the wrong property? And if there was one thing he knew, it was that the owner of the largest plot, a large commercial development company, wasn't going to sell for any amount of money. Brody had done some research, and they were building a small resort retreat. They'd already started working out there.

"No, I'm not sure," Wade admitted through gritted teeth. "But I swear I didn't go that far. This area looks right. It's got to be right."

Heath nodded and started swinging the metal detector over a different segment of land.

"Let's load up and call it a night. We can try again in the morning before it starts to snow."

They each grabbed their shovels and equipment and had started walking back to their four-wheelers when they were suddenly bathed in bright white lights. Headlights.

Wade froze in place like a deer. He clutched his incriminating tools tighter in his fists. Who was it? He couldn't tell. They were blinded, unable to see anything but the bright white orbs aimed in their direction.

Was it the sheriff? No. He wasn't that lucky. He knew the sheriff and could talk his way out of this. The lights were way too high for a patrol car. It was a truck. An older truck, judging by the loud rumble of the engine.

An old truck.

Wade swallowed hard. She couldn't be back already. Not this soon. The ribbon-cutting ceremony was today. Tori would've had to drive straight back after it ended to be here already. She said Monday or Tuesday at the earliest. Why would she have rushed home again?

The answer was on the tip of his tongue, but he didn't even want to think it, much less say it. The way she'd looked at him last night had been different. Something had changed. He'd tried to deny it at dinner, and when he made love to her. He told himself it was just because they both knew it was the end for them.

Wade was a fool to ignore the truth. Tori had fallen in love with him. He couldn't be certain, but maybe she'd decided to come home early before he returned to New York so she could see him again. Or maybe she'd gotten brave enough to tell him how she felt.

And instead she'd caught him red-handed on her property with a shovel and a metal detector. Damn.

Heath leaned in to him, finally daring to move. "Are they just going to watch us or get out of the truck? You think they're calling the cops?"

Wade shook his head. "I doubt it. I think it's Tori."

"Oh, man," Heath said. "I thought she wasn't coming back for a couple of days. What are you going to tell her? You can't tell her the truth."

That was a great question. He'd have to think of something, because the truth was completely off the table. "I have no idea. But you just get on your four-wheeler and go, okay? She and I need to talk alone."

"I'm not going to leave you out here. Doesn't she have a shotgun?"

Wade had forgotten about the shotgun. Hopefully it was locked in the Airstream and not with her in the truck. "Yes, you are. Seriously. I'll be okay. Go, now. It's better that way."

Heath shrugged and turned away from the light to go to his ATV. He loaded his things, cranked the engine and disappeared into the trees. It wasn't until he was gone that Wade heard the truck's engine die. The lights stayed on when the heavy door clicked open.

Wade still couldn't see, but he could hear boots crunching on the gravel. Then a woman's silhouette appeared between him and the truck's headlights. He'd know those curves anywhere.

Tori stopped a few feet away. He was about to say something to explain himself when she suddenly charged forward. Her hand reared back to slap him, and he was going to let her. His hands were full. What was he going to do? Swing a shovel at her? He deserved it, anyway.

Instead, she hesitated for a moment and her hand finally fell back to her side. Tori took a step back, her breath ragged in the darkness. He could finally make out her features in the light. Her eyes were wide, her jaw clenched tight. "You bastard!" she said. "All this time. All those nights we spent together were a lie. You were just using me. Lulling me into complacency so you could slip in and get what you wanted."

"Tori, it wasn't like that." Wade tossed the shovel onto the ground and reached for her, but she took another step back.

"Don't you dare. Don't you try to smooth everything over with your charming lies. I've fallen for enough of those already. I can't believe this." Tori buried her fingers in her hair and clutched her skull. She turned from him and started pacing through the yard like a caged lioness. "I can't believe I let myself trust you when I knew you were the last person I could trust."

"I'm sorry, I—"

"That night in the diner was especially well done," she continued, her sharp tone leaning toward the sarcastic and bitter. "Letting me believe that I'd won. That you had given up trying to take the land from me. And I just ate it up. Watched you with love-stricken doe eyes and sucked up all the crap you threw my way."

"That wasn't a lie. I don't want to take your land. I knew I would hate myself for doing that to you. I couldn't."

"So, what? You decided you'd just wait until I left and steal what you really wanted? Save yourself the trouble and the half-million-dollar expense?"

Wade looked down at the ground, the expression on his face too guilty to be washed out by the bright lamps shining on him. "You don't understand."

"No, I don't understand. And maybe I would, but you've wrapped everything up in a web of lies so thick I couldn't see the truth even if it was right in front of me. What is it that you're after, Wade? It's obviously not the land and your family legacy, as you said before. What do I have on this property that is so valuable to you? What could be so damn important that you would ruin everything…" Her voice trailed off.

Tori's voice trembled at the end, and it made his chest ache to hear her like that. He'd never wanted to hurt her. He'd spent his whole life trying to care for and protect the important people in his life. Why would he want to hurt her? He wanted so badly to tell Tori the truth. But that secret wasn't just his to protect. He couldn't betray his family, even for her. He'd failed his brothers and sister once. Wade absolutely could not do that to them again. No matter how he might feel about Tori. "I can't tell you that. I want to. Believe me, I do. But I can't."

Tori chuckled bitterly and crossed her arms defensively over her chest. "Of course you can't tell me. I can't believe I trusted you. That I let myself fall… *No.*" She corrected herself with a firm shake of her head. "The only thing I fell for was your sob story about family. I'm not about to do that twice."

"Tori, please." Wade reached for her, but she moved out of the way.

She held out her hand for him to keep his distance. "You don't get to touch me anymore." Turning on her heel, she marched back toward her truck. She killed the lights, slammed the door and headed for her trailer.

Wade took a few steps to follow her. He wanted to talk to her. To help her understand.

"You know," she said, "when I was in Philadelphia today, I had started to think that maybe this land wasn't so important after all. I can build a house here, but if the things that make it a home are…somewhere else… what is the point? It seemed so vital for you to preserve your family legacy. So I decided you should. I got in my truck as soon as the ceremony was over, and I came home to tell you that I wanted to sell you the land. And some other things that aren't relevant anymore."

Wade closed his eyes, her words hitting him hard in the gut. She'd trusted him. She cared enough about him to give him the one thing he wanted. And he had ruined it by sneaking behind her back and trying to steal the gift before she could give it. He was an impatient ass, and there were no words in his defense.

"Can I ask one thing? Maybe this is a question you can actually answer."

Wade looked up at her. She was standing on the metal stairs and gripping the door handle with white-knuckled intensity. The patio light illuminated the shimmer in her blue eyes as she watched him. Just the slightest thing could send those tears spilling down her cheeks, but she fought to hold on.

"I'll answer if I can."

"Was all of this just about the land to you? The dinners, the trip to New York, the chocolate-covered strawberries… I know at first it was a game of wits for both of us, but along the way it changed for me. I'd hoped it changed for you, too. Was it all just an attempt to charm me into giving you what you wanted, or did any of that mean something to you?"

Yes, it meant something. He wanted to yell it. He wanted to scoop her up into his arms and kiss her until she couldn't be angry with him anymore. But her furrowed brow and glassy eyes made him wonder if the truth would make things better or worse. Would it hurt her more to know that what they had had was special and he'd ruined it? Or to believe that it all had been a game?

"Tori, I—"

"Wait," she interrupted. "Forget I asked. I think I'd rather not know the truth. Goodbye, Wade."

Wade saw one of the tears escape down her cheek as she opened the door and disappeared inside.

Ten

"You look like hell."

Wade looked up from his desk to see Heath standing in the doorway of his office. He had to admit he wasn't surprised by the impromptu arrival of his youngest brother. He'd been dodging calls, texts and emails from his siblings for over a week. He'd canceled dinner plans at Brody's place. Before too long, he'd figured, they'd send someone to track him down. Since Heath lived and worked in Manhattan, too, he was the obvious stuckee.

Wade looked down at his watch. "Eight days, thirteen hours and forty-two minutes. That means Linda in accounting wins the office pool."

"Very funny," Heath said, coming into the office and shutting the door behind him. "What's going on with you lately? You've been too quiet."

Wade shrugged. "I've been busy. Work always picks

up after the holidays, and it takes a while for everyone to get back into the swing of things."

"Uh-huh." Heath wandered over to the minibar and pulled out a soda from the stash. "Do the other people you say that to actually believe you?"

With a heavy sigh, Wade sank back into his leather executive chair. "No one else ever bothers to ask how I am, so I haven't gotten much practice in yet."

"Tell the truth. How are you?"

"I'm fine."

Heath sat in one of Wade's guest chairs and propped his feet up on the edge of the large mahogany desk. He scrutinized Wade with his hazel gaze as he casually sipped his drink. "Brody was right," he said after a few silent moments.

Wade frowned at his brother. "Brody was right about what? I haven't even spoken to him since I had to cancel our dinner plans."

"Doesn't matter. He was still right. You're in love."

The declaration sent Wade bolt upright in his chair. What did Brody know about being in love? The man was a hermit. "That's ridiculous."

Heath shook his head. "She loves you, too, you know."

"Since when did my entire family become psychic?"

"Mama saw her at the grocery store. Said she was an absolute mess. She's not sure what went on between you two, but she's very unhappy about it."

"I don't date to please Mama. She needs to focus her matchmaking skills on you for a change."

"She shouldn't waste her time," he said with a wide grin. "I'm already married."

"You're hilarious. Keep telling that story and she'll move on to demanding those grandchildren she wants."

Heath shuddered in his seat and took a large swig of soda to wash away the bitter aftertaste of Wade's suggestion. "The point is that she's miserable. You're miserable."

"I'm not miserable."

"You're not Jolly Old Saint Nick, either. You've been avoiding everyone. You've got bags under your eyes large enough to store loose change. Your tie doesn't even match your shirt, man. You're obviously not sleeping."

Wade looked down at the blue shirt and green plaid tie he was wearing. He could've sworn he'd reached for the blue striped one. Must've grabbed the wrong tie and not noticed. Not sleeping for a few days would do that to a guy, he supposed. "I've got new neighbors. They've been louder than usual, and after a few weeks at the farm, I got used to the quiet."

"And it has absolutely nothing to do with the red-head whose heart you broke last week?"

Heath just wasn't about to let this go. Wade knew that if he didn't say something soon, Heath was liable to put him in a headlock and knuckle his scalp until he confessed.

Wade opted to answer the question without really answering it. "She's better off without me."

"Isn't that for her to decide?"

Wade shrugged. "It doesn't matter. She hates me."

"I doubt that. She was just hurt. Your betrayal was that much worse because she let herself fall in love with you."

"She didn't say that."

"Why on earth would she? Anyway, she didn't need to say it. We both know why she rushed home from

Philadelphia. And even if she does hate you now, that doesn't change anything. *You're* still in love with *her.*"

Wade's chest started to ache at the mere thought. The pain had plagued him since the door of Tori's Airstream slammed shut in his face. It had woken him up the few times he had managed to fall asleep. He'd started popping antacids. He'd even done a Google search for "heart attack symptoms" to make sure he wasn't dying. As best he could tell, he wasn't on death's door. He was just in love with a woman who hated him.

"She's never going to forgive me for lying to her. And I can't tell her the truth about what we were looking for. I can't just go to her and tell her I love her and that she's just got to trust me."

"You know, fifteen years ago our lives took an unexpected turn. For the most part we've been able to carry on with our lives. Sure, we remember. Our consciences are burdened with it. We worry we handled it wrong and made a bigger mess of the situation. We pray that no one ever finds out what happened. But for more than twenty-three hours out of every day, I can live my life like it never happened. Can you?"

"Usually. Until I found out Dad sold the land."

"But before that...were you happy?"

Happy was a funny word. Wade didn't like using it. "I was content. 'Happy' sounds like puppies and rainbows. I was pleased with how my life was going."

"And now?"

"And now...I guess, to use your words, I'm miserable."

"We've decided you should tell her the truth."

Wade's brow shot up at his brother's words. "We? Did you all hold some secret council meeting without me?"

"Yes," he said, very matter-of-factly. "Via Skype. We talked it over and decided that you shouldn't give up your chance at real happiness just to protect us."

Wade almost laughed for a moment before he realized Heath wasn't kidding. They had no idea what they were asking him to do. He'd spent his whole life trying to protect them. Trying to make up for that night. He couldn't just flip-flop because they said it was okay. It wasn't okay. "I'm not going to expose everyone, including myself, just for a woman."

"She's not just any woman, Wade. She's the woman you love. Do you want to marry her?"

The image of Tori in an ivory lace gown instantly sprang into his mind. Her red-gold hair was pulled back into an elegant twist. Her peaches-and-cream skin rosy from excitement and champagne. He'd never even thought about it before, and yet the vision of her in his mind was so real that he couldn't push it aside. "If she'd have me."

"Then you can tell her. After the wedding."

Wade opened his mouth, then realized what they had in mind. If he married Tori, he could tell her everything and she couldn't be compelled to testify against them.

"She's not going to marry me unless I tell her the truth. And I can't tell her the truth unless she marries me. So, really, I get nowhere with this."

Heath shrugged. "I disagree. When I came in the door, you were 'fine.' Now you're a man in love who wants to get married. I think you're way ahead. Now you just have to go tell her."

"Yeah, sure. Tori, I love you and I want to marry you. And once you marry me, I can tell you all about how I buried some guy on your property and I'm afraid you'll dig him up while building your dream house."

"Those aren't the words I'd recommend. But if you show up there, tell her you love her, offer her a ring to prove you're serious and explain where you're coming from with all this, I think she'll understand."

Wade frowned at his brother, then turned back to stare at his desk blotter. He'd lain in bed night after night replaying those last moments with Tori. If he'd said or done something else, might it have ended differently? Sometimes the door slammed in his face just the way it had happened. But once, Tori had listened to his words. She'd forgiven him. And that was the time he'd imagined telling her the truth.

He wanted so badly to go back and have another try. Heath insisted he still had a chance to turn things around. He had permission to tell her what she wanted to know, but he wasn't sure if it would make a difference. Could Tori really trust him enough? What if it was too little, too late? Was it possible she was still in love with him after everything that had happened between them?

Wade closed his eyes and pictured Tori as she'd been Friday morning before she left for Philadelphia. Her pale blue eyes were wary, but the love he saw there was undeniable. Maybe he hadn't lost his chance yet. God, he hoped so. He couldn't function like this for much longer. He'd have a real heart attack before too long from the stress and the copious amounts of caffeine he was drinking to compensate for lost sleep.

He had to give it a shot. The gaping hole in his chest begged him to at least try. If she turned him down, he would not have lost anything he hadn't already given away.

Heath looked at his brother. His expression was about as serious as it ever got. "This will work out."

He sure as hell hoped so.

"You always were the optimist in the family." Wade rolled his chair up to the desk with a new fire to put his plan into action. "Okay, Mr. Advertising Executive, direct me to the most environmentally conscious jeweler on the market."

"I should've known—" Heath grinned "—that you would pick the only woman on earth able to resist the little blue box. Let me call one of my guys who handles most of our jewelry accounts. But be warned—odds are it won't be local. You might have to wait a couple days."

Absolutely not. He would be in Connecticut tomorrow, come hell or high water. "That's unacceptable," he said.

"Well, then, get ready to get on a plane."

Wade nodded and rang his admin to clear his calendar for the rest of today and tomorrow. He'd fly to the ends of the earth to get Tori back.

"It's crap. All crap." Tori ripped the sheet of paper off the pad, then crumpled her latest blueprint into a ball and tossed it into the overflowing wastepaper basket. It had to be the hundredth design she'd sketched in the past week, but she hated them all. Even the ones she'd been really happy with before Wade came into her life.

Now everything felt wrong.

Maybe this whole settling-down thing was just a bad idea. Maybe her mother was right when she said that they had a wandering spirit that shied away from the tethers of the typical American dream. A month ago it had seemed like a great plan. She had been bursting with ideas. Fantasizing about her new closet with room for more than five pairs of shoes. Just the thought of a full-size kitchen and an actual living room with a couch and big-screen television was enough to get her blood pumping with excitement.

Now the only thing that set her heart to racing was Wade. And he was long gone, along with the piece of her he'd taken with him.

Tori cussed and flung her pencil across the Airstream. It bounced off her cabinet door and rolled toward the bathroom. She watched it move across the floor, stopping at the butt of her shotgun, which was leaning against the door frame.

It brought to mind the first day he'd shown up on her property. His charming smile. His infuriating arrogance. The way she'd threatened to shoot him. How was she supposed to carry on with her plans when even the sight of her shotgun brought memories of him to mind? Living on his parents' old property would guarantee that she could never get away from Wade Mitchell.

But Tori didn't want to get away from him. She wanted the charming liar back in her arms. She sat staring blankly at her notepad, thinking about what had happened. Since he left, replaying the scene in her mind had given her some clarity. It had allowed her to focus on the words she'd refused to listen to in her anger.

Whatever it was he wanted was important. The land itself had no real value to him, just whatever was on it. Given she didn't even know what it was, it wasn't something she would ever miss. A part of her understood his reasoning. If he could take or move what he needed, Tori could keep her land and they could both be happy. Maybe even happy together.

If only she hadn't decided to come home early.

Tori looked back down at her fresh sheet of paper. The blank squares were taunting her. Picking up a new pencil, she took a deep breath and tried something different. How would she design a house for both her and Wade to live in?

She started with his office. It had an entire wall of windows that opened up on a view of the valley below like the ones overlooking Times Square in their hotel suite. On the opposite wall were floor-to-ceiling bookshelves. A see-through fireplace connected his office to the great room. Both spaces would have twelve-foot ceilings and huge panes of glass. One panel would slide out to let them onto the deck. She sketched in a hot tub where they could sit together in the evenings, talk and drink wine.

Wine… Tori started sketching a dream kitchen with a staircase that led down into a wine cellar. Her pencil moved feverishly now, the rooms flowing together perfectly. Nearly an hour passed before she sat back and looked at the design.

This was the house she wanted. The one with Wade in it. Her gaze moved over the second-story guest bedroom that was right off the master suite. It would be perfect for a nursery. She could just see the ivory-and-green wallpaper, the mobile over the crib. The sunlight that streamed in would provide the perfect amount of natural light. Wade could sit in the rocking chair and read bedtime stories.…

That was the thought that brought the tears to her eyes that she'd fought for days.

Tori grasped the corner of the sketch, ready to rip it off and trash it with the others, but she just couldn't. This was the house she wanted.

The rumbling sound of a car pulling onto her property pulled her attention away from the design. Unable to see from her seat, she got up and walked over to the window.

The corner of a red hood with a BMW logo nearly sent her heart into her throat. She stumbled back against the sink, gripping the counter to keep her knees from giving out under her. Wade had returned to New York a week ago. Why was he here now? To apologize? To offer her more money? Her mind raced with different options, but she shook each one aside. The only way to know for sure was to go out there and find out.

Glancing to her right, she picked up the shotgun and went to the door. She was in love with him, but she was still angry and hurt by what he'd done. He needed to know that.

Tori swung open the door and stepped down into the snow. A snowstorm had blown through the day after she came home, blanketing the property in white and making it impossible for her to look around and search for clues about what he was after.

When she turned, Wade was standing near the hood of his SUV, his arms raised in surrender. In one hand was a bundle of tulips wrapped in florist paper. "Don't shoot," he said with the smile she'd missed.

She raised the gun and studied his face. He looked older, more tired than she remembered. Hopefully he'd had as bad a week as she had. Knowing he might have suffered without her helped soothe her pride a bit. "What do you want?"

"I came here to make you an offer."

It took everything Tori had not to pull the trigger and cover his body in painful welts. An offer? Here she was, designing their home, decorating their damn nursery, and he came here focused on the same old agenda.

"You're too late," she said. "I wouldn't sell you this

land for every dime you have. Flowers won't help, either."

Wade nodded. A flicker of amusement in his eyes sent a flame of irritation through her veins. "That's fine. I'm not here to buy the land."

Tori frowned. "If you don't want my land, what do you want, Wade?"

"I want you."

The intensity in his expression was undeniable. His green eyes were burrowing into her. It made it hard to breathe. He wanted her. *Her.* Not the land. Not what was hidden on it. Her. Her heart leaped in her chest for a moment, but she refused to so much as blink on the exterior. She wasn't going to let him off that easily. "I'm not interested in any more dinner dates. All I got out of that was indigestion and rug burn."

A smile curled Wade's lips. Instinctively she wanted to smile back, but she wouldn't.

"That's okay," he said. "I'm not here to ask you on a date. I'm here to tell you that I'm in love with you."

Tori's hands started trembling, the shotgun unsteady in her grasp. She stood there with her mouth open but without words as Wade came closer.

"Let's just set this down, shall we?" He eased the gun from her hands and laid it in the snow a few feet away. "I'd rather not have our love story turn into one of those tragic tales." Wade handed her the bouquet of tulips. They were her favorite flower. She hadn't ever told him that.

"How did you know?" she asked.

"Brody is a genius. You can find out almost anything with a computer. I've waited seven years to give you those flowers." He put his hands on her upper arms, gently rubbing her skin to warm her. "I've been miserable since we fought. I can't get that night out of my head. I can't sleep. All I can see is the look on your face when you walked away, and it breaks my heart. I'd give anything to see you smile again. Today, and every day of the rest of my life."

If the mention of love wasn't enough, he was making sounds like he wanted to…to…

"I want to tell you the truth. Every bit of it. But it's not just my secret to keep. There are others who could get hurt if the story were to be made public. But I can tell you this much… I was once very young and very stupid. When faced with something no child should have to handle, I made the wrong decision. I believe the evidence of that night is somewhere on your property. I've been doing everything I can think of to make sure no one ever finds it. I've done some things in the past few weeks that I'm not proud of. But I did what I felt I had to do to protect my family. You know how important they are to me. I would protect them with my life, just as I would protect yours. And for now I have to continue to protect their secret, just as I would protect a secret of yours."

Tori could see the pain in Wade's expression. His past was eating at him, gnawing at his gut on a daily basis. She was amazed that she hadn't noticed it before now, but maybe he just kept it too well hidden. He was letting down walls for her. Because she wanted him to. Even if he couldn't tell her everything, he was making the effort. And she could appreciate that. If she could be certain of nothing else, she knew that Wade would do anything for the people he loved. And if he loved her as he said he did, she would be just as fiercely protected.

The sense of security and stability that washed over her in that moment was unprecedented. A lifetime of moving from place to place had never provided it. Even buying this land hadn't provided it. But she'd found it in allowing herself to trust Wade and be protected by him.

"One day, I hope to be able to tell you the rest of the story. And that you'll hear everything I've done and trust me when I say that, right or wrong, I only ever had the best of intentions. I pray for your understanding because you are a beautiful, intelligent woman and I adore you. You make me happy just lying in bed listening to you breathe. I want to wake up every morning to your messy hair and pouty face. And I want to do it here, in Connecticut, in the house you designed."

Tori gasped. "You'd move here?"

He nodded. "I would. There isn't much I can do in the office that I can't do from here with teleconferences and virtual meetings. I might have to go to the city from time to time, but when I do, I want to take you with me. I don't think I like the idea of traveling without my wife."

"But I—" Tori started, then stopped. She watched as Wade eased down onto one knee in the snow. Reaching into his coat pocket, he pulled out a small wooden box wrapped in a gold ribbon. "Wade..." she said, disbelieving. The flowers slipped from her fingers to the snow.

"Victoria Sullivan," he began, unwrapping the bow. He eased open the hinge and held the box up to her. "Would you do me the honor of being my wife?"

Tori glanced down at the engagement ring in his hands. The nearly two carat round diamond was set in a multirow pave diamond band of platinum. It sparkled so brightly with the sunlight reflecting off the snow that she was almost blinded. She had stood in the snow very nearly dumbstruck for the past few minutes, but now she knew she had to find the right thing to say. And it should be easy, since she'd been screaming it in her head since he knelt in the snow.

"Yes," she said, tears pooling in her eyes from the light and the emotions ready to spill out of her.

Wade stood back up, slipping the ring onto her finger. It fit perfectly.

She tore her eyes away from the ring to look up at the man who would soon be her husband. "I love you," she said.

"And I love you." He leaned down to kiss her, almost the official sealing of the deal he'd come here to offer her.

Tori melted into his arms, losing herself in the feeling of being with the man she thought she'd lost forever. Her blood instantly began to heat with the desire he easily stirred in her. Just when she was ready to tug him into the Airstream and make love to her fiancé for the first time, he pulled away and looked down at her with a smug grin.

"Do you have any idea how hard it was to find the perfect diamond for you?"

Tori frowned. "Am I that picky?"

"I don't know if you are, but I certainly am. It had to be perfect. So perfect, I was willing to fly to San Francisco and back to buy it from a jeweler there. This ring is from an environmentally conscious and well-regulated Canadian diamond mine. Certified conflict-free. The band is made of recycled platinum. Hell, the ring box is even made from Rimu wood, whatever that is."

Tori grinned. Wade could have marched right into Tiffany's, bought any ring he wanted, and she would've said yes. But he didn't. He traveled all the way to the West Coast and back to get the ring he knew she would want. That was more precious than the large, flawless stone in the center.

"Rimu is a sustainable wood from New Zealand. And I love it. There isn't a more beautiful and perfect ring in all the world. Absolutely perfect."

"Like you," he said.

Rising on tiptoe, she kissed him again. "Now, let's go inside and get you out of those wet pants."

Wade's brow shot up at her suggestion. He glanced down at the wet knees of his trousers, then back at the Airstream behind him. "Okay, but after that, you need to get back to work designing that house."

"Why?"

"Because," he said, "I'm afraid if I make love to you the way I want to, we're going to roll this sucker down the hill and into a ditch. I need a house. Without wheels. ASAP."

"I'll do my best," Tori said. Taking his hand in hers, she led him over to the Airstream. "Until then," she said, laughing, "if this trailer's a rockin'…"

Epilogue

Two months later

"Remind me again why we're hiding eggs? In the dark?" Tori looked across the silver, moon-illuminated yard at Wade and Brody. They were both chucking the plastic Easter eggs under bushes and behind tree trunks.

Brody straightened and shrugged. "It's tradition. Like watching the Grinch at Christmas. Don't question our methods."

"But there aren't any children to find them."

"It doesn't matter," he explained. "For as long as I have lived on this farm, Wade and I have hidden Easter eggs for the younger kids. I swear to you, if Julianne and Heath wake up and there are no eggs to find, bunny heads will roll."

"You know, when Wade first told me about this, I

thought he meant the Edens hosted a community egg hunt here on the farm. I didn't realize I'd be out in the middle of the night hiding candy for your twenty-seven-year-old brother."

"It's good practice," Wade replied with a wink. "If Mama has her way, there will be grandkids hunting here in no time."

"Yeah, well," she muttered, "I don't know why all the pressure is on me when there are four other kids in this family. We need to get Brody a girl."

"Ha, ha," Brody said flatly. "You're funny. Why don't you get me a unicorn and a time machine while you're at it? Then I can go back to the nineties and gouge my father with the unicorn horn before he could ruin my chances of ever dating."

Tori shook her head and put an egg under the steps of the front porch. Over the past few months she'd gotten to know Wade's family better, including the grumpy and serious Brody. She found that he wasn't really that grumpy or that serious. He had a marshmallow center under that hard-candy shell. It made her want to help other people see though his defenses, as well.

"How do you expect to meet women if you never go out in public?" Wade teased. "Have one ordered on the internet and delivered to your office?"

Brody chucked an egg at Wade. The plastic shell separated on impact with his chest, sending candy scattering across the grass. "I imagine the shipping would be outrageous on that, so no. I have a woman in my life, thank you very much."

Wade retaliated with his own egg. Brody ducked and his egg missed, hitting the tree behind him and flying open. "Agnes doesn't count. She's your fiftysomething secretary. And she's married with grandchildren."

"Don't I know it," Brody complained. "She started making noises a few weeks ago about her anniversary coming up in the fall. She says she wants to take some time off for it."

"That's nice. Are they going on a trip to celebrate?" Tori asked.

"Yes," Brody responded with a heavy sigh. "It's a milestone year. Apparently they've booked a three-week Mediterranean cruise."

"That sounds wonderfully romantic," she said.

Brody shook his head, unconvinced. "Not for me."

"Agnes is Brody's connection to the outside world," Wade explained. "Without her, he's helpless as a babe."

"I am not helpless. There are just some things that I can't do from my office. Or that are easier to have her handle. Like picking up my dry cleaning."

Tori couldn't imagine living in Brody's world without contact with other people. From what Wade had told her, he had a housekeeper who worked at his home during the day while he was gone, but she always left before he got back. And he had his secretary. Aside from family visits, that was it. He lived in seclusion. "What are you going to do when she goes?"

"I don't know," Brody said. He put the last of his eggs in the curled-up nest of the garden hose. "I've been trying not to think about it. I've got months before I have to make a decision."

"I'm sure you can hire a temp from a local agency to come in while she's gone."

Brody frowned at her. "I don't like new people."

"I'm new, and you like me."

"That's because I realized Wade was hopelessly in love and there was no getting rid of you."

Wade came up behind Tori and wrapped his arms

around her waist. She curled against him, seeking out his warmth in the chilly night air.

"You have to keep yourself open to the opportunities around you," he said to his brother. "You never know what you might find. Great things can show up where you least expect them."

Brody looked at the two of them and shook his head. "People in love are disgusting."

"Disgustingly happy," Wade countered, placing a warm kiss just under Tori's earlobe. The touch sent a shiver down her spine that made her want to dump her basket of eggs and drag him back to the Airstream.

"Happily ever after," she agreed.

* * * * *

Don't miss Brody's story,
A BEAUTY UNCOVERED, coming later this year.
And be sure to pick up Andrea Laurence's next book,
A VERY EXCLUSIVE ENGAGEMENT,
part of Harlequin Desire's
DAUGHTERS OF POWER: THE CAPITAL
continuity, in May 2013.

REQUEST YOUR FREE BOOKS!

2 FREE NOVELS PLUS 2 FREE GIFTS!

HARLEQUIN® *Desire*

ALWAYS POWERFUL, PASSIONATE AND PROVOCATIVE

YES! Please send me 2 FREE Harlequin Desire® novels and my 2 FREE gifts (gifts are worth about $10). After receiving them, if I don't wish to receive any more books, I can return the shipping statement marked "cancel." If I don't cancel, I will receive 6 brand-new novels every month and be billed just $4.30 per book in the U.S. or $4.99 per book in Canada. That's a savings of at least 14% off the cover price! It's quite a bargain! Shipping and handling is just 50¢ per book in the U.S. and 75¢ per book in Canada.* I understand that accepting the 2 free books and gifts places me under no obligation to buy anything. I can always return a shipment and cancel at any time. Even if I never buy another book, the two free books and gifts are mine to keep forever.

225/326 HDN FVP7

Name	(PLEASE PRINT)	

Address		Apt. #

City	State/Prov.	Zip/Postal Code

Signature (if under 18, a parent or guardian must sign)

Mail to the **Harlequin® Reader Service:**
IN U.S.A.: P.O. Box 1867, Buffalo, NY 14240-1867
IN CANADA: P.O. Box 609, Fort Erie, Ontario L2A 5X3

Want to try two free books from another line?
Call 1-800-873-8635 or visit www.ReaderService.com.

* Terms and prices subject to change without notice. Prices do not include applicable taxes. Sales tax applicable in N.Y. Canadian residents will be charged applicable taxes. Offer not valid in Quebec. This offer is limited to one order per household. Not valid for current subscribers to Harlequin Desire books. All orders subject to credit approval. Credit or debit balances in a customer's account(s) may be offset by any other outstanding balance owed by or to the customer. Please allow 4 to 6 weeks for delivery. Offer available while quantities last.

Your Privacy—The Harlequin® Reader Service is committed to protecting your privacy. Our Privacy Policy is available online at www.ReaderService.com or upon request from the Harlequin Reader Service.

We make a portion of our mailing list available to reputable third parties that offer products we believe may interest you. If you prefer that we not exchange your name with third parties, or if you wish to clarify or modify your communication preferences, please visit us at www.ReaderService.com/consumerschoice or write to us at Harlequin Reader Service Preference Service, P.O. Box 9062, Buffalo, NY 14269. Include your complete name and address.

Navy SEAL Blake Landon joins this year's
parade of *Uniformly Hot!* military heroes in
Tawny Weber's

A SEAL's Seduction

Blake's lips brushed over Alexia's and she forgot that they were on a public beach. His breath was warm, his lips soft.

The fingertips he traced over her shoulder were like a gentle whisper. It was sweetness personified. She felt like a fairy-tale princess being kissed for the first time by her prince.

And he was delicious.

Mouthwatering, heart-stopping delicious. And clearly he had no problem going after what he wanted, she realized as he slid the tips of his fingers over the bare skin of her shoulder. Alexia shivered at the contrast of his hard fingertips against her skin. Her breath caught as his hand shifted, sliding lower, hinting at but not actually caressing the upper swell of her breast.

Her heart pounded so hard against her throat, she was surprised it didn't jump right out into his hand.

She wanted him. As she'd never wanted another man in her life. For years, she'd behaved. She'd carefully considered her actions, making sure she didn't hurt others. She'd poured herself into her career, into making sure her life was one she was proud of.

And she already had a man who wanted her in his life. A nice, sweet man she could talk through the night with and never run out of things to say.

But she wanted more.

She wanted a man who'd keep her up all night. Who'd drive her wild, sending her body to places she'd never even dreamed of.

Even if it was only for one night.

And that, she realized, was the key. One night of crazy. One night of delicious, empowered, indulge-her-every-desire sex, with a man who made her melt.

One night would be incredible.

One night would *have* to be enough.

Pick up *A SEAL's Seduction* by Tawny Weber, on sale January 22.

Evangeline is surprised when her past lover
turns out to be her fiancé's brother. How will she
manage the one she loved and the one
she has made a deal with?

Follow her path to love January 22, 2013, with

THE ONE THAT GOT AWAY

by Kelly Hunter

"The trouble with memories like ours," he said roughly, "is
that you think you've buried them, dealt with them, right up
until they reach up and rip out your throat."

Some memories were like that. But not all. Sometimes
memories could be finessed into something slightly more
palatable.

"Maybe we could try replacing the bad with something a
little less intense," she suggested tentatively. "You could try
treating me as your future sister-in-law. We could do polite
and civil. We could come to like it that way."

"Watching you hang off my brother's arm doesn't make me
feel civilized, Evangeline. It makes me want to break things."

Ah.

"Call off the engagement." He wasn't looking at her. And it
wasn't a request. "Turn this mess around."

"We need Max's trust fund money."

"I'll cover Max for the money. I'll buy you out."

"What?" Anger slid through her, hot and biting. She could
feel her composure slipping away but there was nothing else

for it. Not in the face of the hot mess that was Logan. "No," she said as steadily as she could. "No one's buying me out of anything, least of all MEP. That company is *mine,* just as much as it is Max's. I've put six years into it, eighty-hour weeks of blood, sweat, tears and fears into making it the success it is. Prepping it for bigger opportunities, and one of those opportunities is just around the corner. Why on earth would I let you buy me out?"

He meant to use his big body to intimidate her. Closer, and closer still, until the jacket of his suit brushed the silk of her dress, but he didn't touch her, just let the heat build. His lips had that hard sensual curve about them that had haunted her dreams for years. She couldn't stop staring at them.

She needed to stop staring at them.

"You can't be in my life, Lena. Not even on the periphery. I discovered that the hard way ten years ago. So either you leave willingly…or I make you leave."

Find out what Evangeline decides to do by picking up THE ONE THAT GOT AWAY by Kelly Hunter. Available January 22, 2013, wherever Harlequin books are sold.